THE VIRGIN SCORECARD

A COLLECTION OF NOVELLAS

LAUREN BLAKELY

ALSO BY LAUREN BLAKELY

Big Rock Series

Big Rock

Mister O

Well Hung

Full Package

Joy Ride

Hard Wood

Rules of Love Series

The Rules of Friends with Benefits (A Prequel Novella)

The Virgin Rule Book

The Virgin Game Plan

The Virgin Replay

The Virgin Scorecard

Men of Summer Series

Scoring With Him

Winning With Him

All In With Him

The Guys Who Got Away Series

Dear Sexy Ex-Boyfriend

The What If Guy

Best Laid Plans

The Feel Good Factor

Nobody Does It Better

Unzipped

Always Satisfied Series

Satisfaction Guaranteed

Instant Gratification

Overnight Service

Never Have I Ever

PS It's Always Been You

Special Delivery

The Sexy Suit Series

Lucky Suit

Birthday Suit

From Paris With Love

Wanderlust

Part-Time Lover

One Love Series

The Sexy One

The Only One

The Hot One

The Knocked Up Plan

Come As You Are

Sports Romance

Most Valuable Playboy

Most Likely to Score

Standalones

Stud Finder

The V Card

The Real Deal

Unbreak My Heart

The Break-Up Album

The Caught Up in Love Series

The Pretending Plot (previously called *Pretending He's Mine*)

The Dating Proposal

The Second Chance Plan (previously called *Caught Up In Us*)

The Private Rehearsal (previously called *Playing With Her Heart*)

Seductive Nights Series

Night After Night

After This Night

One More Night

A Wildly Seductive Night

ABOUT

Indulge in this collection that begins with Mr. Right Now and Captain Romance -- two romances between virgins and athletes that complete the bestselling RULES OF LOVE series.

Mr. Right Now

I've got a problem. After a dozen failed dates - but who's counting - I'm done hunting for Mr. Right. I'm more than ready to cash in my V-card, and at this point I'll gladly hand it over to Mr. Right Now. When I go out with my friends for a night on the town, I bump into the perfect candidate. A guy from my past who kissed like a dream but took off before we could say goodbye. The swoony, charming pro athlete is back in the city and he's as ready to help me with my project as he is to win baseball games. The next morning, I'm deliciously satisfied and I know I've chosen wisely. But when he leaves again, I can't stop wondering -- what if Mr. Right Now is actually Mr. Right? And how do I get him back?

Captain Romance

I don't have luck on my side when it comes to romance. That's why I'm laser focused on my career as a sports reporter and making a mark as a woman in this tough field.

When one of the city's baseball stars asks me to spend a night on the town, I have to draw the line. Just friends, I say.

He's good with that.

Very good with that.

So good that I start falling for my new friend.

Of all the swoony, charming, thoughtful men in this big city, why is the one I want thoroughly off-limits? But if I want a chance with the guy they call Captain Romance, I'm going to have to put more than my heart on the line.

This collection also includes Kiss Your Tulips, Limo Bang, and DogFishing, three stories set in the Rules of Love world.

THE VIRGIN SCORECARD
A COLLECTION OF NOVELLAS

By Lauren Blakely

Want to be the first to learn of sales, new releases, preorders and special freebies? Sign up for my VIP mailing list here!

MR. RIGHT NOW

A VIRGIN SCORECARD NOVELLA

1

SHANE

New city. Fresh start.

That's what I'm about these days.

If I were a betting man—I'm not—I'd wager all my chips at the tables tonight. Everything's been going my way since I got on the plane in New York six hours ago. We took off bang on time, I landed in my once-upon-a-time hometown early, and now my luggage is popping out of the baggage carousel first.

I grab the black bag and head to the Lyft already waiting outside the airport.

Yep, bet it all on red.

The driver scurries out of the sleek black car, but I wave him off. I traveled light—always do. Baggage isn't my style.

"I'm all good, mate. I'll just set it in the back seat," I tell him as I toss my bag in the car.

The bearded man with the San Francisco Dragons ball cap peers at me a little longer than a driver normally would. His brown eyes flicker a few seconds later.

Given the telltale hat, I've got a hunch why.

He points at me, a delighted smile curving his weathered face. "Are you . . . Shakespeare?"

I laugh as I slide into the seat. "I am indeed."

"Holy fireman," he says, then rushes to the driver's side, starts the engine, and peels off into traffic. "Dude. You are everything we need, Shakespeare. I am so stoked the team traded for you."

I smile as I pop my seat belt on. "I'm pretty chuffed too."

"Chuffed," he snickers. "I can't get enough of it. The British-isms. By the way, huge Dragons fan."

"I gathered as much," I say, gesturing to the purple air freshener in the shape of the team's logo. It hangs from the rearview mirror.

"But I've seen more heat in a toaster than in the Dragons bullpen. Been writing letters to Ms. Winters for the last year, begging her to get us a fireman," he says, naming the team owner for the baseball franchise as he cruises away from the airport. "Everyone knows you can't go all the way unless you have a fireman." He slaps a meaty paw against the dash to make his point. Can't say I disagree. He peers in the rearview mirror, a grin lighting his face. "And we got one. Shakespeare the Fireman. Hey, can I call you that?"

"Have at it. I pretty much answer to any variation of Shakespeare," I say, since that's the nickname that's stuck with me since I played for the LA Bandits three years ago. I started with that team, then was traded to the New York Comets for a stretch, and now I'll be suiting up for the Dragons. "The only variation I'm not fond of is 'Shakespeare, you suck,' which is what opposing teams' fans call me."

"Screw them. You're our Bard now," the driver says, proud and possessive.

"Thank you. I also answer to Shane."

He cracks up as he steers the car onto the 101. "Shane, you're *our* anomaly. Brilliant, chuffed, bloody fabulous," he says, imitating my accent.

Not well, but that's beside the point.

Also, I don't care if a fan talks *British* to me, as has become the saying among the so-called Shakespeare crew. It's part of my *anomaly factor*, and I don't mind it.

"You're the twenty-ninth English dude ever to play in the majors," he remarks, almost as if he's citing intel from my Wikipedia entry.

"That is correct," I say, and since he's a fan, I don't need to dive into my story. It's a simple one, and like many good stories, it's a love story. My father is a Hall-of-Fame American pitcher—Jedd Walker. He led the league in shutouts and innings pitched thirty years ago, won a couple of Cy Youngs and a World Series. When he retired, he traveled to England, met a brilliant woman in a pub, fell in love, and shacked up with her in London.

And the birds and the bees made me a little later—helped along by a pint or two, I'm sure.

After thirteen years in London, my parents moved back here so I could play baseball in America, a decision that served me well, that gave me the team skills to become a major leaguer.

The driver and I chat more about the Dragons' chances this season as he cruises the car into the city, the lights of San Francisco flickering like fireflies against the night sky.

I draw a deep breath, energized to be here again, where I lived as a teenager.

I had my first kiss here—under the bleachers at a ballpark with a charming, adorable pixie of a blonde, the kind of girl you could lose your mind for. The kind I nearly gave my heart to. Probably would have if we'd had more time.

What's she up to these days?

Does Clementine still live here?

I shake the thought away. I'm not here to track down my high school sweetheart. In fact, I ought to stay far, far away from women and romance, given my recent track record.

Best to focus on work.

"Good to be back," I say, gazing out the window into the night.

It's also good to be out of New York and the troubles I escaped from. Trouble with an ex.

So much trouble my agent sat me down at The Lucky Spot in Chelsea and told me a few weeks ago, "Romance and baseball don't always mix. You're heading into the arbitration end of this season, so when you return to San Francisco, maybe don't hit the concert scene, since everyone you meet there is bad news."

Well, one person was bad news, so I get where his worry comes from. It's his job to worry, and romance has a way of knocking a man off-kilter. Especially when it goes tits up.

So I won't do the concert thing, even though finding new bands is a hobby of mine. But that's fine. I take off for spring training in a few days, so I won't have time to attract trouble before I go.

The driver exits the 101 into the city, and I breathe a sigh of . . . second chances.

Maybe my agent is right.

It's always best to focus on work, especially when you're entering a contract year and you have new employers to impress. Like Marlow Winters, the no-nonsense owner of the San Francisco Dragons.

My goal is to make sure Marlow and the rest of management can't imagine a team future without me. I'll convince them with my steely attitude in the ninth inning, my wicked right arm, and the fireballs I can pelt over the plate.

That's all I need—strikeouts and saves.

We reach my new home in the Marina, a third-floor beauty overlooking the bay with a fantastic view of the Golden Gate Bridge. The driver pulls up to the curb.

"Had a blast driving you tonight, Shakespeare," he says, scuttling around to open the door and grab my bag. "Screw your courage to the sticking place," he booms, quoting *Macbeth*.

It's a thing some fans do.

And I love it.

"And we'll not fail," I say, completing the quote. "Have a good night."

As he pulls away into traffic, I head to the gleaming white door of my new pad. I tap in the code and go inside, then head up the stairs to my floor.

I snagged this place last month, right after I learned of the trade. Already feels like home.

It's modern and clean, with black and gray furniture and framed posters of my favorite bands. I hung them up when I was here last month visiting friends before I officially moved.

Setting the bag down, I flick on the rest of the lights and wander through my new home, heading to the bedroom to savor the view of the bay—one of this rental's many selling points, as well as the young, hip neighborhood.

Another benefit? It's an entire country away from Tinsley.

I shudder at the thought of my ex.

The night we met at a club at the end of last season, I'd fallen for her, hook, line, and sinker. But she had only fallen for my *rising star*, and soon enough, the gossip-talk-show host latched on to bigger stars, landing an A-list actor and ditching me.

In. That. Order.

She's history as of a few weeks ago, and I hope I've learned my lesson. Don't give your heart away to people who'll stomp on it.

Heading to the kitchen to grab a glass of water, I unlock my phone.

I'm antsy. I don't relish being alone. I like company and friends, going out, having a good time.

I open a group text to some of my local mates.

Shane: I have arrived. Let the fun begin.

Drew: Gee, I was waiting for you. Twiddling my thumbs. And here you are, saving the day.

Sullivan: Life has been sad and empty without you . . . *Not.*

Shane: Figured as much. But that all changes tomorrow.

Sullivan: Yes, this new band is in town. Secret Frog Lovers Mate in the Night. Wanna check them out?

Shane: Would love to, but alas, I can't. Promised my agent, like I told you. But the comedy club you suggested still works.

Drew: Seriously? Are we really sticking to that plan?

Shane: Do you not like to laugh? A comedy club is the perfect way to welcome me back to town.

Sullivan: Yes, Drew, we're going to the comedy club. Case closed.

Shane: Listen to the Cougar.

Sullivan: You wish you'd been traded to the Cougars.

He's not wrong. I'd lose my mind to play for the team that won the World Series a little more than a year ago. And I'd love to have a ring like Sullivan. Someday.

For now, though, I want to do three things. Have a good time. Impress my employers. Don't fall in love again.

That's it.

That's all *this* ballplayer can ask for.

2

CLEMENTINE

I have a theory that one of the best spots to meet a hip, cool guy is at a comedy club. But not just any night of the week. I'd like to meet this dream man the night a female comic performs.

It's a litmus test. A lot of guys subscribe to the patently false idea that only men can be funny.

As if.

So if a man's digging a comedy show headlined by the fairer sex, he's passed the first test.

No sexist pigs need apply to date me.

Or bang me either, but one step at a time.

At my home in Cow Hollow, I lift a glass of champagne to toast with my lady pack as Taylor Swift serenades us from my phone.

"To the best dates anyone could ever ask for," I tell Erin, Frankie, and Nova.

Because even though I'm going to Stella's Comedy Attic *tonight* to celebrate the next phase of my dating life, that new era starts *tomorrow*. I don't expect to meet a leading candidate to deflower me while at a comedy club with my girlfriends on Galentine's Day.

Taylor hits a high note, and Magnus yips.

He's part of the pack—the only boy member.

I bend down to scoop up my Papillon rescue into my arms. I smooch the six-pound beast's soft, silky head. He licks my cheek.

"So this makes us an official foursome tonight?" Erin deadpans, tipping her glass against mine as she flicks a strand of chestnut hair from her shoulder.

Peering over her red heart-shaped glasses, Frankie lifts her flute too. "What else is Galentine's Day for but a foursome?" she chimes in with a sly grin. "Come to think of it, I believe someone wrote that on a card today at my shop."

I laugh. "What sort of flowers did they order for that?"

"Stargazer lilies, of course. They work best in fours," Frankie says, deadpan, as if she gets this request at her flower shop all the time.

Nova clinks her glass to mine. "I'll say this though— foursomes are tough, friends. We're talking lots of choreography."

Laughing, I knock back some bubbly, grateful to spend this silly love day with my best friends before I put a saddle on the dating horse tomorrow. "I'll trust you. Besides, who needs a boyfriend? Not this gal," I shout as my playlist shifts to P!nk, the ultimate girl-power singer.

"Not this gal either, that's for sure," Nova says dryly. Nova does everything dryly. She's the queen of deadpan.

"I know, babes, so no gal-hunting for you tonight," I tell her, wagging a finger.

She rolls her dark-blue eyes. "I'm out with the three of you. Who is going to hit on me?"

"You never know. And if someone hits on *me*, I'll be all *Nope, not tonight, not any guy, no how*," I say, since I'm ready for what tomorrow might bring.

The wreckage of the last few years of dating disasters is behind me.

I won't let the litany of over-and-out men from the apps get me down. Not the guy who dated me so he could store Omaha Steaks in my freezer, not the dude who asked me to shave his balls after we'd only had one latte—I told him ball shaving required a five-course meal plus a delish dessert—and not the fella who showed me photos of all his ex-girlfriends.

Who happened to look like my long-lost twins. Ew.

Over the last few years, I've never made it to the five-date mark with a single one of them. That's my demarcation point for getting busy between the sheets.

Or really, it *was*.

But I'm turning over a new leaf, and after tonight's celebration with my besties, I'll put myself out there again. I'll get back on the apps and roll back the five-date line to just . . . one.

Fine, maybe two.

Three at the most.

I swallow more bubbly. "I'm done with waiting for the right guy for a relationship. Clearly the five-date rule is a lie. After Galentine's Day"—I glance at the black cat clock on the wall, its tail keeping time—"I'm implementing the one-to-three date rule."

Nova rolls her eyes. "Just do it, Clem. Just get some dick once and for all."

"Dick down, dick down, dick down," Frankie chants, and my jaw falls open.

"Sources say our heroine is ready to hit the apps tomorrow night," Erin booms in her best on-air voice, a thing she uses a lot since, well, she's a sports reporter. "All witty, dog-loving five-and-ups in the looks department in the city of San Francisco . . . on your marks."

"Five-and-ups," Nova says with an approving nod. "You're casting a wide net, Clem."

"I'm open-minded. I'm not obsessed with looks. I just want a nice guy with a big heart. I even told Sierra to keep her eyes peeled for me at her bar. Well, when she gets back from her Valentine's Day trip with her hubs," I say.

Erin places a finger on her lips. "Shhh. Do not speak of Valentine's Day tonight. It is *only* Galentine's Day."

I take another drink. "Or really, the *eve* of my new dating plans. And this time on the dating merry-go-round, I'm not looking to get serious or to have a relationship. But if he's a good guy, I *might* let him into my pants," I say, shimmying my hips suggestively.

Erin bumps her hip with mine. "Someone is determined to rip up her V-card any day now."

I'm ready to say goodbye to my virginity. I've banged enough vibrators to know I want the real thing at last. And I've dated enough duds to know I just don't need to wait for big love anymore.

I set down my glass to shake my fist at the sky. "Thanks, Stephen Scott. Hope you're enjoying having ditched me."

Frankie looks at me, concern painted in her eyes.

"I'm kidding, hon. I'm so over my ex. He's history. One in a long string of terrible . . . dates. But I am the queen of terrible dates no more," I call out.

Erin clears her throat. "And we got you a sash to that effect."

I blink. "Seriously? You got me a sash?"

"Yes. This is your one-month celebration." Erin whirls around, grabs her purse, and fishes around in it till she locates a white ribbon. "Ta-da."

"No, you didn't," I say, holding up a stop-sign hand, since did she really?

And the answer is . . . yes, she did.

"Wear it, girl. Wear it with pride. Own it," Erin says, brandishing the sash.

I can't even with my friends. But a girl's gotta do what a girl's gotta do.

I step into the center of the circle of awesome and dip my head.

Erin clears her throat. "By the power vested in me as one of the fab foursome, I pronounce you DTF."

"Woo-hoo. Clem is Down to Fuck," Frankie adds.

I arch a brow at the crudely drawn words written in

lipstick on the white material. "'Screw Mr. Right. I'm looking for Mr. Right Now,'" I read aloud.

Yep. Sounds about right.

Let the new era of dating begin.

3

CLEMENTINE

My parents have a great marriage, and so does my older sister. And I read a dating survey a few years ago that said the longer you wait to have sex, the longer the relationship. So I'd deemed the fifth date as the ideal time for me to have everything I might want in romance—sex and love in the same person.

A win-win!

Double first name notwithstanding, Stephen Scott seemed like Mr. Right. I was sure he'd be the one to cross the line to get in my pants. But with my schedule training dogs and his schedule as the king of the outdoors, our first four dates were spread over several months, since he'd embarked on a Mount Everest climb. When the fifth date approached upon his return from the summit, he declared he'd had an epiphany at the top of the world—he *only* wanted to use his body for *more noble pursuits*.

"My body is a temple, and I won't soil it with sex," he'd announced.

Fabulous.

Fucking fabulous.

Between that and the fact that he didn't dote on Magnus as much as I'd have liked—fine, he scratched the guy's chin, but he never kissed him—it was clear he was not the man for me.

Men like him are my past.

I set Magnus on the couch so we can take off for the club. "Be the best boy in the world," I tell him.

He folds his paws then lets his tongue loll out. Gah. Could I have a better dog? I think not.

I scratch his chin. "Yes, I know you are the best boy."

He tilts his face, and I drop another kiss to his head, then we leave and make our way to the club.

Once we sweep into Stella's, I take off the sash. It's adorable, but I'd rather not advertise my hot-to-trot status.

We grab a table near the stage, and after the waiter asks us for our drink order, Erin gasps.

"What?"

She drops her voice to the barest whisper. "That's Hudson Tanner," she mouths.

"Who's that?" Frankie asks, crinkling her freckled nose.

"I swear you never know a thing about sports," Erin says with a laugh.

Frankie arches a wry brow. "You never know a thing about flowers," she tosses back.

Nova drags a hand through her thick red hair. "Which is why we're all such a fab foursome. We support each other."

"Anyway, he's the Cougars owner," I say to Frankie.

"And look who he's with," Nova whispers. "Marlow Winters. She owns the Dragons, and she's a fox."

Nova's spot on. The billionaire brunette is quite pretty, in a classy, I-own-a-private-jet-drive-a-Bugatti-and-live-in-a-mansion way.

But soon, the server returns with our drinks—Diet Coke for me right now—and we turn to the stage. After the opening act warms us up, the headliner strides onto the stage, looking all Zooey Deschanel quirky cute as she entertains us with tales of the challenges of dating in a swipe-right culture.

"Has this ever happened to you?" Matilda begins. "You check out someone's dating profile, look at their pics, and oh my God, you see the cutest shots. I mean, I fell in love with this one image. You would too. I swear you would. He was brown and tan, had big bat ears. What? It could happen to you. Chihuahua min pins are so cute."

I crack up.

And I'm not alone.

Across the room comes a loud, deep snort.

I whip my gaze in its direction.

All I can make out is the profile of a tall twentysomething man sitting several tables away. He holds his belly, laughing.

He reminds me of someone, but I can't quite make out who with the light dimmed for the set.

"Hey, it happens. Dog fishing is a real thing," Matilda says, finishing the joke.

The guy snorts even louder.

I wish the lights were brighter, but I put him out of my mind.

I'm not here for a man—I'm here for my gals. So I sit back and enjoy the rest of the set with my friends.

When the set ends, Nova spots someone she interviewed for her Badass Babe podcast, so she drags Frankie over to say hi.

I grab Erin's arm, and we make our way to the bar. "Promise me you won't let me talk to any of the total cuties, the hotties, or the even remotely good-looking guys who didn't think Matilda was the funniest act ever," I tell her. "I refuse to be swayed by a man with no sense of humor."

"A good sense of humor is basically kryptonite," Erin says.

"I know! That's why I liked Stephen Scott. He was funny enough—until he got all enlightened."

Erin makes a shushing gesture with her hand, snapping it like a duck's bill. "No ex talk. It's forbidden."

I mime zipping my lips. Then I throw away the key.

"Good. Now, repeat after me," Erin says.

I pretend to reach for the key and unzip my lips again. "Am I allowed to speak now?"

"Yes, but no talk of exes who decided to put their body to more noble use," Erin says.

"You're right. You're so right. Because do you know what the most noble use of all is?" I ask, then take a dramatic beat. "Sex. So much sex."

She rolls her eyes, laughing. "You're the most perverted virgin I know."

"Why, thank you very much, and yes, I am. But I will *not* give it up to an unfunny guy."

My friend arches a brow. "You want me to put handcuffs on you right now? So you don't accidentally pick up someone here who doesn't share your sense of humor?"

"Do you carry your own handcuffs? I always suspected you were the type of girl who was prepared for kink at a moment's notice, you naughty vixen."

"As if. But: confession. I like to keep a scarf in my purse, so I figure that'll do if I need to be tied up pronto."

"A thin little scrap of silk that you could toss around your neck but also be tied to the headboard with. Cha-ching. That's what I'm talking about," I say, licking the tip of my finger and touching the air so it sizzles.

When we reach the bar, I do a double take. Wait, make that a triple take. Then my pulse speeds up as my gaze lands on a pair of warm hazel eyes.

My mind races back in time. Images flicker before me. Memories of red-hot kisses behind the bleachers.

Sexy stolen moments after baseball games.

A touch here, a caress there.

A man I haven't seen in more than seven years.

The guy at the end of the bar with the dark-blond hair and mischievous gaze crooks his lips up into a grin.

Before I even have time to take a breath, he's striding toward me, closing the distance in a heartbeat.

Shane Walker.

"Of all the comedy clubs in the city," he says when he reaches me, and . . . that voice.

Fuck me with a high-powered fourteen-speed dolphin that rocks my world.

His accent is even sexier than it was when we were in high school.

Duh. I hope so. He's got seven years on the eighteen-year-old hottie that he was.

The British baseball player.

The flirty, dirty, gorgeous guy with the accent *and* the prowess on the diamond.

Now, he's even sexier, his voice rumblier, his whole look just . . . hotter.

"Shane Walker, you're supposed to be on the other side of the country," I say, wagging a finger at him.

"And I was. For a bit. Now I'm here. How the bloody hell are you? You look fantastic, Clementine."

The way he says my name with that British lilt is like a dose of lust, and it goes straight to my panties.

Hey, libido, settle down. We're not getting off the bench till tomorrow.

Erin clears her throat. "Hi there."

I straighten my shoulders, recovering some composure. "This is my friend Erin. This is Shane Walker. He was a pitcher at my high school."

Erin smiles. "I certainly know who he is now. The former closer for the New York Comets. Brand-new closer for the Dragons—something the team desperately needs."

"And I am at their service."

"I hope they have many opportunities to use you," Erin says. Then she whispers to me, "I hope you can use him too."

I swat her, but she just giggles.

Erin excuses herself for the ladies' room and makes like the wind, while Shane turns his hazel-eyed gaze just on me. "That was a fantastic show tonight. Did you enjoy Matilda? I legit laugh-snorted through most of it."

My eyes widen. "Are you serious? Was that you? The snorter?"

Shane shrugs, owning it. "Yep. I am a certified snorter. I'm that person."

"I heard you straight across the club. I kept wondering who had the adorable laugh-snort."

"Oh, it's fetching, I'm sure," he says doubtfully. "That's what you dream of, right? Finding a bloke who snorts when he laughs."

Honestly, I kind of do. I dream of a funny bone. A big, inviting sense of humor. A huge heart. But though I'm a dreamer, I know better than to serve all that up, so I keep my answer simple. "I do," I say.

Shane smiles. "You found him."

My heart flutters unexpectedly as his eyes lock with mine. "Good. And the laugh-snort is totally fetching. Completely," I say with a flirty grin, then a happy sigh.

"Then it's my lucky night." He looks at me a little like he did years ago, yet in a whole new way too.

Like how a man looks at a woman he wants.

I flash back to our plans, to our teenage dreams that didn't come true.

I have definitely dreamed of what might have been with this sexy man.

And I'm not sure I want to wait for tomorrow to get started on my new dating plans.

4

SHANE

My *almost* prom date looks absolutely fantastic. Her big green eyes are welcoming, with a saucy sparkle in them. Her hair is short, platinum blonde, and held back with a little hair clip. I sneak a glance at it—a small dog with big butterfly ears is emblazoned on the side.

Definitely must ask her more about that later.

Tight jeans cling to fantastic legs, and a black top slopes off her shoulder, revealing creamy skin with a constellation of freckles that I would like to trace with my tongue.

Clementine Rose was the kind of pretty in high school that made me sneak glances at her behind me in calculus. Now, she's the kind of pretty that makes it impossible to look elsewhere.

She's all grown up and deliciously sexy.

"So what have you been up to? It's been ages since we said we were going to go to prom," I say, since that was the last time we talked.

She frowns. "There was no prom at the Carter Club for us."

I smile, a little wistful too, and it's not because I wish I went to that cheesy event space with her. "And I still wish there had been."

"But you had such a wonderful opportunity. And look where it landed you. Now you're a superstar," she says.

"I'm not sure I'd say superstar," I say. I'm not being falsely humble—that's true. Yes, I am rising in the sport of baseball, but I'm only three years in. I might be cocky with my teammates, since that's how we roll, but outside of the locker room, I'm more of a realist.

"You don't have to. I did. And I'm not wrong. I can smell it on you like a cologne," she says playfully, sniffing the air.

"Yes, I did douse myself in Superstar before leaving my home. Smells like . . ." I wave a hand, casting about for an analogy for the fake cologne brand I just made up, then snap my fingers. "Ten-thousand-dollar bills."

"Hey, do they even still make those?"

"Why did they ever make them?" I ask. "Literally, what is the point of a ten-thousand-dollar bill? Who wants to carry one around? Do you want to be the chump who leaves your ten-thousand-dollar bill in the cab or the loo?"

"The point of them is to show that you have it. It's like the monetary equivalent of unzipping your pants and whipping out a monster cock. Amusing, eye-open-ing, perhaps even highly entertaining." She raises a finger to finish her point. "But a totally unnecessary sideshow."

I crack up. "Did you just say 'monster cock'? Did you truly just say that?"

Her pink lips part in an O, and she clasps her hand to her mouth. "I did. How utterly naughty of me. Wash my mouth out with soap."

Bloody hell. Clementine is flirty. Clementine is also dirty. Maybe even bawdy. Was she this naughty in high school? Or is this a new thing?

"You have a naughty side, Clementine," I say.

"Does it bother you, Shane? Would you prefer I be more . . . dainty?" She's like a strawberry cocktail, chased by a shot of tequila—sweetness and fire.

"I prefer *you*," I say, since two can play at this flirting game.

That's all this is.

Simple bar flirting.

Nothing more.

There's no time in my life for *more* anyway, but maybe tonight I can enjoy a few moments with her.

The girl who got away once upon a time.

I gesture to the bar. "Drink, love?"

She nibbles on the corner of her lips, a soft laugh falling from her lush mouth.

"What are you laughing at?" I ask.

"You still say '*love*.'"

I shrug, a little helpless. "You can take the boy out of England, but you can't take the England out of the boy."

"Good. I like the England in the boy," she says, then

cocks her head to the side, appraising me. "Or, really, the man."

Is this happening? Did I truly walk into a comedy club on Valentine's Day and bump into the one woman who never quite left my mind?

I wasn't planning to meet anyone tonight. I was planning to do the opposite—*not* meet anyone.

"And this man likes being right here, right now," I tell the flirty blast from my past.

"Good. Very, very good, you *snorter.*"

I laugh, something I haven't done a lot of when it comes to dating, and women, and romance.

Brilliant. Fucking brilliant.

I'm already thinking of her in ways I shouldn't.

Romantic ways.

I should say, *Nice to see you. I start spring training in a day*, but then again, what's the harm in chatting with an old friend from school?

This is simple catching up. There's no harm.

None at all.

But there's one little matter I need to be clear on.

"So, when we order this drink, will your boyfriend show up in a few minutes, and is he a six-foot-ten professional MMA fighter who will toss me out of here?"

"Don't be silly. He's over seven feet, and he's also a bounty hunter."

"No problem, then."

She sets a hand on my arm. "Besides, you can just throw him one of those wicked fastballs of yours."

"Ah, I'll challenge him to a baseball duel. Perfect."

She smiles, full wattage, an all-the-stars-in-the-sky grin. "And your girlfriend?"

"Like your giant fake boyfriend, she doesn't exist. So can I get you a drink?"

"I'd love a martini."

"And I'll have the same," I say, and we move to a spot at the far end of the bar. When I catch the gaze of a blonde bartender, I raise two fingers.

She strides over, flashing a grin. "What can I get you?"

Her voice is full of my home country, but now's not the time to chitchat with the bartender from London. I place our order, then the woman turns to my . . . friend.

Who feels immediately like my date.

"Your hair clip is the cutest thing ever. Is that a Papillon?"

With a delighted smile, Clementine lifts her hand, running a finger across it. "I'm in mad love with them. I have a rescue Papillon, and he's the love of my life."

"As it should be with a dog," the bartender says, then taps the counter. "I'll get to work on your drinks."

She heads down the bar, and I turn to Clementine, eager to hear all about her. "So, what are you up to now?"

"Try not to be shocked," she says, deadpan.

I square my shoulders, schooling my expression. "I'm putting on my *unsurprised* face."

"I'm a pet trainer, mostly dogs," she says proudly.

I tip my forehead to the clip. "That's perfect for you. Didn't you have ten dogs growing up? A whole passel?"

She shoves my elbow. "Just two. Nowhere near enough."

"Naturally. One can't have enough dogs."

"You get me."

"And business is . . ."

"It's great," she says, then whips out her phone, clicks to Instagram, and shows me her feed—picture after picture of her working with small beasts.

Leading classes.

Teaching agility.

Wow. She's not simply a dog trainer.

She's a celeb of sorts. Her feed is brimming with local influencers, sports stars, news anchors, tech wunderkinds. "You're the dog trainer to the stars," I remark.

"I work with everyone. I just have a few high-profile clients," she says, downplaying what's clearly a booming business.

I click on one of the pics and scroll through the comments. I arch a brow. "And it says you have a waiting list several weeks long. Good on you, Clem."

She smiles graciously. "I can't complain. Work has been good to me. And it's been good to you, Mister Wicked Fastball. To think, it all started with your championship game senior year." She punches my right arm.

A pang of sadness digs into my chest, but it's chased by happiness—that's how I felt as we were winding down at the end of high school. She was the only thing I missed when I took off for an unplanned baseball tournament, and the chance to start college early that summer.

"I can't believe I had a championship game clear across the country the weekend I'd asked you to prom," I say with a sigh.

I'm back in time, eighteen again, finishing school, sneaking off to kiss a beautiful girl after a game. Clementine and I went out a few times, made out a couple more times, and made plans.

The woman in front of me pouts, over-the-top and adorable, as her pink lips curve down. "And to think I was left all alone, standing in the corner of the Carter Club ballroom in my emerald-green dress, no one to dance with."

The image is beautiful and breaks my teenage heart all at the same time. I tuck a finger under her chin. "Somehow I doubt you were left standing all John-Hughes-rom-com-movie-style in the corner."

Clementine shrugs, a little coquettishly, those big green eyes full of mischief. "What do you think happened, then?"

"No doubt all the blokes asked you to dance," I say, imagining the scene now. A long line of hopeless and undoubtedly horny boys, eager for a shot at the most captivating girl in school. Eighteen-year-old me is weirdly jealous of those sad sacks, even seven fucking years later.

"Ha," she says with a laugh. "Not exactly. Also, aren't John Hughes flicks a little old for you?"

"Yes. But I've spent enough time on planes and in hotels in the majors that I've tried to watch pretty much every film made in the last thirty to forty years."

"That's some serious commitment to sampling entertainment."

"Music, movies, and books are kind of my thing. But what about you, calling me out? Isn't John Hughes too old for you too?" I counter.

"Yes! But my parents went on and on about those movies when I was growing up, so finally, for a girls' night last year, my friends and I tried watching the holy triumvirate—that's *Sixteen Candles*, *Pretty in Pink*, and *The Breakfast Club*."

"The verdict?"

"We turned them off and watched *The Adventures of Mister Orgasm* instead."

"You can never go wrong with a fictional cartoon hero committed to a woman's pleasure," I say as the bartender returns with our drinks.

"Here you go," she says, and I pay for them straight-away, thanking the blonde behind the bar. Then I turn to Clementine, lifting my drink.

"Something we couldn't have done in high school," I say.

She leans a little closer, dipping her voice to a whisper. "Unless we were very sneaky."

"We were kind of sneaky, weren't we?"

"We had our moments, slipping behind the bleachers for no particular reason other than that it was fun to kiss there," she says.

I pick up the thread easily, warmth skimming down my body from the memories, or perhaps it's from the present moment with her. Maybe both. "Stealing a kiss before the bell rang," I murmur.

"See? We might have been sneaky at prom too," she says, her tone a little seductive.

"Were you going to slip a flask between your breasts?" I ask, taking the liberty to set a hand on her forearm.

Her breath catches as her gaze drifts down to my hand. Then her eyes swing back up, meeting mine. Her irises shimmer with desire.

"Shane Walker, you naughty man." She glances around, checking our surroundings, then lowers her voice more. "Maybe I was. Just for you to discover. Does that make you miss prom even more now?"

"Like you wouldn't believe," I tell her, stroking her wrist. She trembles as I touch her, and her reaction makes me never want to stop.

"Such a shame, then," she says, a little breathy.

We're both talking about the night we missed and about the here and now.

Funny how I came to this club to avoid the temptation of meeting a woman at a concert.

And here I am, reconnecting instantly with *this* woman.

She inches closer. "And there was no John Hughes moment for me at prom. In the end, I didn't go. I went out with girlfriends instead. We did karaoke in Japantown, then went to a diner, and we had a blast."

"Good," I say, and now it's not eighteen-year-old me who's relieved—it's *this* me.

What the hell is going on? Do I truly care that much about my high school girlfriend's whereabouts one night in June seven years ago?

Maybe I do.

"So you don't have to worry about the long line of tongue-wagging teenage boys wanting to hit on your ex," she adds.

Busted.

Thoroughly and completely.

Though she doesn't quite seem like an ex. An ex is someone you broke up with or who dumped you. Clementine and I wanted to continue, but circumstance pulled us apart.

"Was it that obvious that I'm a jealous bastard?"

Her eyes swing down to my hand again, touching her wrist, then return to my face. "Completely. But rest assured, there were no stolen kisses, no flasks, and no third base in the Carter Club coatroom, complete with mothballs."

A rumble works its way up my chest. "Clementine Rose, you're reminding me of all my favorite teenage memories with you. Except for the mothballs."

"Mine too," she says, then shifts her hand, palm up, inviting me to thread my fingers through hers.

I do, our fingers sliding together, sending an erotic charge straight down my spine.

I can only imagine what trouble we'd have gotten into at prom. And I can definitely picture the best kind of trouble tonight. "We were good at the good kind of trouble," I say, lifting my martini glass with my free hand.

She clinks her glass to mine. "Should we toast to good trouble?"

But that hardly seems enough. This night is

sparkling with possibility, teasing me with the prospect of the best kind of evenings.

"To good trouble and to stealing kisses," I offer.

She licks her lips, flicking her tongue along the corner of her mouth.

I groan, unbidden.

Let there be good trouble tonight.

Surely I can handle good trouble.

It's only love I need to avoid.

That's what I tell myself as we toast.

"I'll drink to both of those," she says, with a sexy smile that makes my heart flip.

Harder than just a good-time flip.

5

SHANE

One martini later, and her hand is still in mine.

And our fingers and thumbs are practically fucking.

Okay, not exactly.

Fingers fuck in other ways. But the way she skims her soft hand along mine fries my brain.

Trips my senses.

Reminds me of all the other what-ifs we missed.

Not simply prom.

But something else we talked about then . . .

She was going to come to my championship game, but the tournament was switched at the last minute from San Francisco to Miami. I spent two weeks there before heading off to college, also in Florida. Two weeks I was going to spend with her.

Circumstance, the cockblocker.

"I missed seeing you at the championship game too. It was supposed to be held right here in the city. I was looking forward to that. Which makes me a selfish fucker, I suppose."

She lifts a brow in question as she settles into a seat at the bar. "You wanted me at your game?"

I've only had one drink. So it's not the martini going to my head. It's her. "I wanted *you*."

"I wanted to be there, Shane. At the ballpark by the water. Cheering for you," she whispers.

"I would have loved that," I say, clasping her hand tighter as we inch closer.

"You always seemed to enjoy it when I went to your games," she says, taking me back to some of my favorite memories.

Back then, when I had romance *and* baseball. When my favorite thing—the sport I loved—was tied up with the girl I was quickly falling for. The two hadn't become dangerously entangled like they did last season with Tinsley in the bad kind of trouble. The kind of trouble that turned into distraction, lies, and heartbreak.

Tinsley's the last thing I want to think of though.

And it's remarkably easy to shove her out of my mind, since I only have room in it for Clementine right now. In fact, in this corner of the bar, it feels like we're the only two people in the world.

"I used to love closing out a game and finding you in the stands after a save," I tell her.

"Kissing me after your victory," she recounts, and she is talking my language.

"I missed that most when we won the championship. Can you believe that? I had everything I thought I wanted then—a fast track to the majors—but I was dying, fucking dying, to kiss you after that win," I say, and it all spills out in a heap of wishes and wants.

Ones that her eyes seem to reflect back at me. They shimmer with hope.

"Mmm. I loved your kisses, Shane Walker. I wanted more of them. I wanted . . . other things with you too," she says, letting me connect the dots, and I absolutely do.

"Fine. I wanted to do much more than kiss you too," I say, a dirty hum in my throat.

"Mmm. You mean . . . more than third base?" She nibbles on the corner of her lips.

I laugh, then loop a hand around her waist. "My lovely Clementine, I wanted to hit a home run with you," I whisper.

"I wanted that too," she whispers, then in a softer, barely-there voice, she adds, "Want that tonight."

And I wave the white flag.

Not that I was doing a good job resisting her, but I've zero intention of that now. "Can I kiss you?"

"You better," she says, squeezing my fingers harder, tugging me closer here at the bar, guiding my hands to her hips. Happy to have them there.

It's so public, and we're on display.

But I don't care one bit about that.

I stand, and she stays seated on the stool, parting her legs ever so slightly.

I move in between the V of her thighs, sliding closer, enjoying the heat radiating between our bodies. I gaze into her green eyes, shimmering with lust.

Then I cup her cheek, brushing my thumb along her jaw.

Her breath comes in a quick pant.

And all at once, I recall perfectly how she likes to be kissed.

Clementine Rose likes to be taken.

Holding her face, I drop my lips to hers. A soft murmur greets me as I shut my eyes and capture her mouth with mine.

She stretches her neck, giving herself, offering her mouth.

And I take it, kissing her gently.

Her body melts under my touch, her hands looping around my neck.

She's like an old-time Hollywood starlet, all glitter and dreams.

And that's the kind of kiss I give her—a silver-screen one. The kind where the heroine leans back and lets the hero lead.

But her hands play with the ends of my hair, and her sexy little sighs say, *Keep going, give me more.*

Her subtle body language asks to be swept away.

To be consumed.

That's exactly what I want to do with my high school sweetheart, especially since kissing her feels not quite like coming home . . . but more like stealing home.

She's a dream to kiss, a woman wanting all that I have to give.

And I want to give.

I want to give her anything she wants.

Not because I'm magnanimous.

Please.

I'm a man lusting after a woman, craving her body, her lips, her pleasure.

Her.

I want to give her everything because I'm greedy too. I want all the things she seems to be offering by the way she's moving, arching her body, sliding her tongue tenderly along my bottom lip, then whispering, *"More,"* against my mouth.

That's my cue to go full black-and-white movie with her. I kiss her like she's the woman I've come home to after all this time.

Like we're crossing the years, erasing them.

We're reconnecting with our lips and mouths, with breath and touch.

With heat and desire.

I deepen the kiss, stroking my tongue against hers, exploring her. I lose myself in the sweet, decadent taste of her mouth and all her vibrant Clementine-ness.

She pulls me closer, her fingers tangling in my hair, her lips hungry.

In a heartbeat, she sits up higher, then scoots off the stool. And holy fuck, she drops her hands from my hair, grabs my waist, and jerks me close. In a quick switch, she's suddenly kissing me hard and hungry, like she'd be devastated if we didn't fuck tonight.

Join the club, Clementine.

Fucking join it.

I've got to have her.

She presses her lithe body against mine, groaning into my mouth when she rubs against my erection, and yes.

Time to go.

Absolutely time to ditch this bar.

I'm about to break the kiss, catch my breath, and invite her home when she wrenches apart from me, then says, "Come over tonight."

And I'd like to thank the baseball gods for trading me to San Francisco.

"Yes," I say. That's the only answer.

But not quite so fast.

"I need to say goodbye to my friends," she says, sounding like she's coming up for air, collecting her thoughts.

"I suppose I should do the same," I say, though Sullivan and Drew won't give a flying fuck.

Still, when Clementine strolls to the tables near the stage, that gives me a chance to sit down, let the blood divert to other parts of my body.

Perhaps the brain.

There. A minute or two later, I'm not sporting the evidence of her effect on me, so I make my way to say goodbye to my mates.

I reach their table, interrupting a debate on Elmore Leonard versus Raymond Chandler.

"Chandler," I declare, since bar debates can be entered at any moment.

"Give your reason," Sullivan demands, sounding and looking like Ryan Reynolds.

"He was an American and a Brit. Naturalized as a British subject," I say.

The darker-haired Drew scoffs. "That's a selfish reason. It's all about you, isn't it, Shakespeare?"

"Speaking of me," I say with a wicked grin, since why hide the thrill of tonight? "I'll see you at spring training.

Well, you," I say, pointing to Drew, since he's my Dragons teammate. I pat Sullivan on the shoulder. "And we'll see this poor tosser when we destroy him on the field."

"There will be no destruction of the best team in baseball," Sullivan says, then tips his forehead in the direction of Clementine, who's chatting with three women. "Didn't take you long to decide romance was back in the cards, bud?"

Drew sets a hand on his heart. "So cute that you found a woman on Valentine's Day. I'm gonna write a poem for you."

I play it cool, scoffing. "Who said anything about romance?"

Sullivan rolls his eyes. "You're so pathetic. You're smiling like you just saw your long-lost lover."

Am I that transparent?

Perhaps I am.

Maybe I need to remind myself that I'm sitting on the bench.

Love isn't part of my San Francisco plan. I refuse to fall for anyone. No matter how easy it'd be to fall for her. I'll have to tell her I'm not in the market for romance. That I need to focus *only* on baseball. That tonight is just one night.

I'll tell her in the Lyft, and if she's looking for something longer, I'll say goodbye to her at her door, à la gentleman that I am, then head on home. Only fair to put my cards on the table.

"I've got everything under control," I tell the guys. "Just like I do when I come into the ninth inning."

"Always cocky underneath that *I'm so likable* exterior," Drew teases.

"All right, fuck off, you sad sacks," I say, then smile when Clementine weaves through the crowd on her way to me.

"Dude, you're so far gone already. Look at your goofy grin," Sullivan says, too loudly for my taste.

"See you at spring training, arseholes," I say, then start to head to the exit. But before I turn away, Drew catches the eye of a brunette, then says to Sullivan, "Hey, that's Erin Madison. The local sports reporter you've been hot for for the last year."

My eyebrows shoot into my hairline. "And the plot thickens," I say to the guys, then shift gears when Clementine arrives by my side.

"Ready?" I ask the woman I want to spend the entire night with.

And maybe more.

Settle down, heart. You're taking a break.

But my heart thumps harder when her eyes lock with mine, and she answers me with "More than you can ever know."

Pretty sure my plans are going tits up.

In every way.

6

CLEMENTINE

Clearly, fate is my friend tonight.

My brand-new bestie.

There's no other explanation for kismet dropping *this* man into my orbit twenty-four hours before my plans to fling myself into the Battle Royale of Tinder dating and mating.

Sure, I'll still enter the ring, but bumping into Shane Walker on *Dating Eve* is like drawing a winning hand in Vegas.

He's not only an ace—he's all four of them.

But I also know it's only fair to give him the 411 on my lady sitch. Sure, my virginity is truly *only* my business, but I'm also big on honesty. It's not a secret I want to hide from him. I'd like him to know, just in case sex gets weird.

Nerves prickle across my skin, racing up my neck as we slide into the Lyft, and I gird myself. I practice what to say like I practice my dog training tips before seeing a new client.

I've been training dogs for years, but every pooch is unique.

Don't worry. He'll get the hang of it.

What a good boy!

Yup. I'll just mix them up a bit.

I've been training with vibrators for years, but I bet your dick is one in a million.

Don't worry. I'll get the hang of it.

What a big cock!

There. I can do that. I can definitely say all that.

Except . . . Shane is kind of a ten. Fine, he's totally an eleven.

Ugh, will he be turned off?

Turned on?

Freaked out?

I have no idea.

Guys are strange. Sometimes I do think they are aliens, wrapped occasionally in hunky packages and shot in pods from the hulls of spaceships to vex straight ladies here on Earth. Like, can we possibly ever figure out how to talk to men in the same language?

I swear dogs are easier to understand.

But I've got to try with Shane.

I want my bad luck streak to end, and I want it to end tonight.

Trouble is, my throat is dry now that we're zipping through the city, hell-bent on Pound Town.

He's quiet too, looking a little lost in thought as we sail along Bay Street.

That's not good for a V-card partner.

"So," I begin, hunting for words as I scan the too familiar sights.

"So," he adds, sounding a little awkward too.

Oh shoot.

Is he getting cold feet?

That would be just my luck.

"Did you, um, miss the city?" I ask, then want to smack myself. I've spent the last hour with him making flirty, dirty talk. Now, I'm regressing to *small talk*?

"I did. It's good to be back," he says, then rubs his palms along his jeans. A sign of nerves too.

Yup. He's losing interest.

We've entered the small-talk zone. Where sex dreams go to die.

Shane clears his throat. Here it comes. The letdown. *Three, two, one.*

He points out the window at the Luxe Hotel, a gorgeous, chi-chi place that opened a year ago. Maybe he wants to escape in his pod and fly to a room there on the top floor. "Wait. Wasn't that . . .?"

Ah, that's easy enough to answer. Perfect conversation topic to get the flow going again. "Yes, that was the once-upon-a-time Carter Club. They razed it when the Luxe Hotel came to town. No more mothballs. No more seventies cheese. All the shag carpets in the hall are gone. Now it's trendy and hip, with purple velvet chairs in the lobby and too-cool-for-school artwork and low lights, and there's a lounge with all sorts of fantastic cocktails with names like Gold Rush and Mining Country," I say, and fuck a duck. I'm going on about a hotel now.

Shut up, Clem.

"So clever," he says, adding a chuckle, and that feels fake.

The flow is not flowing.

How has this delicious night gone to hell already?

What happened?

I retrace our steps, trying to pinpoint the moment we turned into the Awkward Zone. Let's see. Back at the club, after our swoony kiss to end all kisses, I said come over, he said yes, we saw our friends, and we got in a car.

Wait, did something happen with his friends?

Maybe that's it?

"Anyway, where do you live?" he asks, breaking the awkward with . . . more awkward. Since it's his Lyft app we used. We entered my address into his freaking app. He knows where I live.

I fix on a friendly smile. "Cow Hollow," I say, gesturing to the driver's phone. "You know, where we're going and all."

He smacks his forehead, a little embarrassed. "Right, right. Of course. A bit daft for a second there," he says, and he's not the Shane of ten minutes ago.

He's someone else.

A male alien. A male-lien.

Or maybe he's like Steak Guy, and he wants to check out my freezer first for meat storage before he lets me down.

What would I do if a dog training sesh went off the rails?

Think, Clem, think.

I got it!

"That's okay. We can try again," I say, in my best peppy trainer voice, like I'm talking to a stubborn Chihuahua.

Shane jerks his gaze to me. A line creases his brow. "What?"

Oops. That was the wrong strategy too.

Nothing is working. No wonder I'm the queen of terrible dates. *I* am a terrible date.

"I don't have a big freezer," I blurt out.

And fuck ten million ducks.

It's official. I'm clearly the reason I don't make it to the fifth date. Here I am on the first date with an amazing guy, and I don't know how to handle a single thing, including . . . *talking.*

But maybe my former high school boyfriend does, since a sly smile sneaks across his handsome face. "Do you need to freeze something, Clementine? Or is that just your secret code for wanting to stop and get some ice cream?"

In one quick retort, he's back to fun, flirty Shane.

A cue for me to return to fun, saucy Clem?

But the foot I shoved in my mouth is still lodged uncomfortably in the back of my throat, and as the Lyft driver—a lovely brunette who doesn't speak—slows at the light, I unspool all the worries I've built up in the last several minutes.

"I'm the queen of terrible dates," I confess, all the words spilling out. "I've had a string of comically bad dates for the last few years. So bad they belong in a joke book. I dated a guy who wanted to check out my freezer for steak storage. Someone else asked for a twofer—he wanted to take me out for a latte *and* get dog training advice for an unruly Yorkie. Another guy brought his mom on the first date. I kid you not," I say, holding up a hand like I'm swearing an oath.

Shane exhales, all calm and cool. Then he places a palm on my leg, and oh, that's nice. I like his touch. It's easing my nerves.

"Let's tackle each of those," he says. "My mom already met you at a baseball game years ago. Thought you were great, so she won't be popping over tonight. Plus, not my style. Second, I don't have pets, so don't need a training twofer, but someday I'd like a cat, and I plan to name him or her Lennon, and if he or she poses any trouble, I'll just ask the internet what to do. And three, I promise I have a very large freezer and zero interest in ice-cold steaks."

I let out a huge breath of relief for all of that, for every word of his lovely reassurance, but I'm not done. Not even close. "Good. But those guys are nothing compared to the last guy I went out with. Everything was going swimmingly with him. I liked him a lot, then he climbed Mount Everest, said he wanted to use his body for more noble pursuits, and he no longer wanted to have sex at all with anyone," I spit out. "And that really bummed me because I think I would like sex. Like, *a lot.*"

Shane's hazel eyes brim with shock. "I can't even imagine a more noble pursuit than sex. Or, frankly, than the pursuit of female pleasure." Then he stops, lifts a hand, blinks several times, and shakes his head. "Wait.

Hold the bloody hell on. Did you just say you *think* you'd like sex?"

That question makes landfall right as the world's most silent rideshare driver pulls to the curb. She shoots us a cheery grin in the rearview mirror. "Here we are. Good luck with your sex talk. I hope this drive was as good for you as it was for me. How about a five for five?"

I guess she makes up for in listening what she lacks in talking.

"Thanks. I'll be sure to give you five stars," Shane says, then we unbuckle and scoot out of the car, standing under a streetlamp outside my home. My maybe-sorta-I-don't-know-what-he-is-anymore date lasers his eyes on mine. "Let me ask that again, Clem, now that it's just us. Did you just say you think you'd like sex?"

And . . . he hates virgins.

Clearly.

We're no longer heading straight for Planet Bed, where the male-lien and the Earth girl will play *Take Me to Your Penis.*

Still, I'm a woman who knows her mind, and it's time to woman up. No more galloping brain or blurty mouth.

I know what I want.

Honesty, trust, and a little nooky.

Time to say the whole truth.

I square my shoulders, lift my chin, and take a breath. "Yes, I did say that, because I like the idea of sex. I think about sex a lot. I like to watch videos of men making women feel incredible in bed. I like to get off to thoughts of what that might feel like when someone else does that. I want to know what sex feels like. Ideally, good sex. I'm a virgin, but I'm not innocent. Not one bit." I tap my temple. "So yes, I think about sex a lot, and I also think I'd *really, really* like it."

I expel a big breath, a lot relieved, but there's more to say. I gear up for round two as a smile tips the corner of his lips.

That emboldens me and so do his words when he rasps out in a smoky, knee-weakening voice, "You don't sound too innocent, Clementine. Not one bit."

That's all I need to keep going. "I just haven't met the right guy—someone I want to sleep with. I want someone who's funny and thoughtful and reasonably attractive, but I'm not looking for a relationship. Not at all. So please don't think I'm waiting for Mr. Right," I say, borderline imploring both for him and for me. I can't quite read his response though—a furrow creases his brow, and his eyes turn more intense, but he stays focused, clearly listening. "I've been there, done that. I've tried. I'm so over trying, Shane. Honestly, at this point, all I truly want is Mr. Right Now. I'm twenty-five, and I thought I wanted to wait to have sex till I was in a serious relationship, but I can see that isn't going to happen, and I'm super okay with that." I smile and shrug lightly, easily, so he knows how very okay I am with no strings. "I don't need more, I don't need commitment, but I would like more of your body tonight. I'm still incredibly turned on from how you kissed me, and I'd really like to sleep with you with no expectations." I take a beat, draw a final, fortifying breath, then finish with my official request. "If you'd like to sleep with me too."

There.

I did it.

I put myself out there in a big, scary way.

That was harder than writing a dating profile.

Than swiping right.

Than sliding into a guy's DMs.

That was telling my truth to a guy I—*gasp*—actually care about.

I wait for his response, but not for long.

His smile is a constellation lighting up the night sky. "I would love to be your first. I'm pretty sure I'd be great at being Mr. Right Now, because I was going to tell you, too, that I'm not in the market for a relationship. I wasn't quite sure how to say it, and that's why I went a little quiet in the car. I'm sorry if that worried you."

That's why he went silent. That makes sense now.

"I'm not worried," I say, my shoulders relaxing, my overactive pulse settling. I'm curious, though, so I stay silent, waiting and hoping he shares more.

"It's just . . . well, you've been so patently honest with me, and I want to be the same," he says, and it sounds like this is hard for him, and I want to tell him it's okay, I'll listen. Instead, I do that—listen. "I just got out of a bad relationship in New York. Where my heart was a little bit broken. She didn't think I was good enough, or rich enough, and she left me for someone with a bigger star and a bigger name, and I don't want to go through that again," he tells me, vulnerability coloring his tone, and I just want to hug him, and to hiss at her. Who would do that to this fantastic catch of a man? "I can't tell you how refreshing it is, Clementine, that you just put what you want on the table." An embarrassed laugh bursts from him. "Holy hell, I'm spitting out words too." He scrubs his jaw, laughing.

I giggle, bouncing on my toes. "It's infectious, isn't it? Confessing what you really want?"

"Evidently it is," he says, then loops a strong arm around my waist. "So I hope you're good with all that."

I tap my chin. "Gee, sounds like neither one of us wants strings. I'd say we're on the same page, and that's very, very good."

He grins. "Yes, but let's correct one thing."

I slide closer to him, savoring the connection again. "What's that?"

He strokes my jaw, sending a shiver through me. "Reasonably attractive? I'm reasonably attractive?"

I laugh, then shake my head. "The only one more handsome than you is my dog."

He hums. "I accept. Now, let me take you upstairs because I think you'll *really, really* like sex too, because I *really, really* want to sleep with you and introduce you to the joys of fucking."

"Let's go," I say, and neither one of us is speaking male-lien.

After all these years, all those duds, I'm finally ready to lose my virginity.

Bring it on, Mr. Right Now.

7

SHANE

That didn't help matters at all.

Wait. Back that up.

Her confession helped matters in my trousers. But I didn't need a leg up there. I was, and still am, ready to go in that department.

The trouble is my stupid heart.

It's beating faster for Clementine.

Thumping harder.

It's not fucking supposed to. I told my heart to stay in time-out. It's wounded. It's taking a break. It's on the bench.

Yet it's hungry for this woman.

For more than no strings.

As I follow her up the steps, I ought to just focus on the gorgeous sex offer she laid out. The one I accepted. Only, I like everything she just said so much. I like *that* she said it. Her openness is an allure. Honesty is such a turn-on, for my dick evidently. But, inconveniently, it flips the switch on the organ in my chest too.

Settle down, heart.

There. A stern talking-to will do the trick.

I wish.

She's just so easy to like. Easy to fall for. When she reaches the door, she swivels around, an impish look in her pretty eyes. "Oh. I have to warn you, if my dog doesn't like you, it's lights out."

"Your canine holds the key to your knickers?"

She laughs. "Well, that's fair, right? If he doesn't like you, there's a clear reason."

She's not wrong. Dogs are excellent judges of character. "Clearly. I'll do my best to gain his approval."

As she opens the door, there's a scratching sound behind it, then a happy whine once it swings open.

The whimpers grow louder, and a tiny beast jumps up and down on his back legs, greeting his person. "Hey, big guy. Of course I missed you," she says, scooping up the white-and-brown fluffball and kissing him. She turns to me. "This is Magnus."

The tiny Papillon tilts his head and opens his snout like he's considering giving me a verbal dressing down. "Be good," she warns him.

And he behaves, sitting taller in her arms, closing his snout.

"Hey there, Magnus," I say, then stroke his chin.

His tongue lolls out, and since when in Rome . . . I bend and drop a kiss to his silky head.

He answers by licking my cheek. A sloppy dog lick from jawline all the way to my eye.

Converted!

Clementine hoots. "Shut the front door! You're in."

She steps back, wagging a finger. "Admit it. You clearly covered your face in liverwurst."

"It was bacon." Then I gesture to the hook that holds a leather leash. "I presume he needs to go to the loo. Let's take him for a walk down the street?"

That earns me a preposterously large grin from the pixie blonde. "Are you trying to get in my pants by being good to my dog?"

Stroking my chin, I study the ceiling for a few seconds. "Well, you already promised me your knickers, so at this point, I'd say I'm just that great a guy."

She rises on her tiptoes and brushes her lips to my other cheek. "You are."

Then, she hooks a leash on her pup, and we head back the way we came. As we wander down the pavement, we chat, catching up more as we go.

"So if your ex was a jerk, because she totally was for saying you're not good enough, since you're freaking amazing," she says, "and all my dates were jerks, does that mean we're each other's only good exes?"

"Funny, I was thinking something along those lines at the club."

"You were?"

Magnus stops to sniff a tree, and we both slow our pace. "Yes, except . . . we aren't truly exes, are we?"

She tilts her head in question. "We're not?"

I nudge her with my elbow. "We never actually broke up. Life got in the way."

"Hmm," she says, seeming to noodle on that as Magnus finishes and we spin around. "You're right.

There was no dumping. So no anger or true heartbreak."

I wouldn't say no heartbreak, but now's not the time to protest on that count. "And honestly, we probably would have kept going," I say, then I catch my breath, a little surprised I said that. "Did I just get ahead of myself by presuming we'd have kept on?"

She laughs, setting a hand on my arm. "Shane, we would have kept on in every way, especially at prom. I wanted to keep seeing you, and I also wanted to see you naked," she says, then waves her hand at my chest. Her voice goes low, seductive. "I wanted all this unreasonably attractive hotness. And I still want it now."

We practically race back to her place.

Five minutes later, she unclips the dog's leash and sends him to the couch. "Stay, Magnus."

Obediently, he curls up in a dog ball.

"Bye-bye," she says, waving to the beast, then she pulls me into her room and shuts the door.

She slides her hands up my chest. "Hi, you."

"Hi to you, Clementine Rose," I murmur, then dip my face to her neck, pressing a kiss to her soft skin. She smells like oranges and honey. The former is fitting for her name, the latter for her personality. I can't get enough of her scent, and I kiss her neck so thoroughly, she's sighing and moaning when I reach her ear and nip on her earlobe.

"Shane," she whispers on a breathless pant.

I pull back, meet her heady gaze, then run a finger across her lips. "I'm so damn glad I ran into you this evening."

"Me too. Can you please undress me and take me tonight? Now. I can't wait any longer."

She removes her hair clip, and I make quick work of her top, then undo her jeans. She helps me along, sliding them down her legs, stepping out of her boots. I step back and whistle in appreciation for her lacy black panties and matching bra. The set is so damn sexy, it's almost a shame to remove them.

But it's time for them to go.

I roam my hands around her back and undo the bra, all while I dust tender kisses on her lips and eyelids, then let the fabric fall to the floor.

I haul in a harsh breath at the lovely sight in front of me. Perky tits, soft, creamy skin, and a flush down her chest.

The best part though?

The way she bites her lips then gasps as I cup her tits. Groaning at the glorious feel of her flesh in my hands, I knead harder, teasing at her already firm nipples.

Her hands fly to my hips, grabbing me tight. "Can I take your clothes off too?"

"Seems fair," I tease, and in seconds, I'm down to my boxer briefs.

She tugs at the waistband, a fantastically filthy look in her green eyes. A look that turns hotter, needier when she squeezes my hard-on.

"Oh fuck, that feels good," I grunt as she strokes my dick over my briefs.

She grins like she's won the lottery. "Monster cock," she whispers with the wildest grin.

I crack up. "If you say so."

"I do, I do, I do."

Then she handles the rest of the stripping, yanking on my boxers till they're gone. Her lips part in a wild O as her gaze lands on my cock—thick, hard, and pulsing for her.

"You seriously have a . . . beautiful dick," she says, her voice husky, her eyes reckless.

"I'm so glad you approve of my package," I tease. "Now, enough admiring of me. I need to worship your pussy with my mouth."

"Let the service begin," she says, and flops onto the bed.

I climb over her, shimmy those knickers down her ankles, then moan in lusty appreciation at the sight.

My Clementine is soaked.

She's fucking glistening, and I need to savor all that sweetness. I kneel between her legs, spread her thighs, and run my hands along the soft flesh. "You're so fucking edible," I growl as I stare at her sweet, hot, and perfect pink center.

As she arches her back, her hips rise. Already, she's asking for me with her body, and her need makes my dick thump hard.

But the pursuit of her pleasure comes before mine.

I lower my face and kiss her legs, dusting soft lips along her thighs, inching closer to the heady paradise. Taking my time, I lavish soft kisses on her thighs, her mound, then closer, and so much closer.

When I'm there at last, she's begging, gasping, and finally, I press a kiss to her pussy.

We both groan at the same time.

She tastes incredible—all desire and bare need.

I lap up her wetness, swirling my tongue around her clit, drawing dizzying circles that make her rock and arch against me.

Her hands fly to my hair. She grips me, tugging me closer.

I love how in touch she is with her own body. With her own lust.

It drives me—her noises, her gasps, her fingers that curl around my head.

"Yes, oh God, yes," she cries out as I suck on her clit, flicking my tongue against the delicious rise.

Then I press an openmouthed kiss to her, devouring her with my lips as she moans and writhes.

Soon, she thrusts with wild abandon, and I kiss her like crazy as her voice reaches the night sky.

In one long, glorious gasp, she calls out, "*Yes.*"

Then comes, shuddering beautifully.

As her taste floods my tongue, I kiss her gently till she seems to come down from the cliff of bliss. Then I let go, sweeping my lips along her mound, her stomach, her pert breasts.

I raise my face, meeting her eyes.

They're shimmering with lust, and satisfaction too. "That was a joy indeed."

"More joy where that came from, love," I rasp out.

A faint blush spreads on her cheeks from the term of endearment.

Or maybe from the orgasm.

Hard to say, and really, who cares right now?

I push up on my elbows. "Have you thought about how you want it for your first time?"

"I want you on top of me. Just like this. And I have condoms."

"It's good to be prepared," I say, as she reaches into the nightstand and produces one.

I shift to my knees, but before I slide it on, she sits up, reaches for my cock, then curls her fist around it.

Lust surges down my spine.

"Like I said, monster cock, and I can understand the appeal of the ten-thousand-dollar bill now," she says with a grin.

I crack up, loving that we can laugh in this moment.

It's amazing and wildly dangerous because laughing like this leads to falling.

Falling fast.

8

CLEMENTINE

Breathe.

Just breathe.

But I also stare, since, well, there's a gorgeous man between my legs.

Hallelujah.

He's so much more than looks though. So much more than his carved jaw, strong cheekbones, than his warm eyes and lush lips, than his ten-thousand-dollar cock.

Shane Walker is a man who's caring, witty, and honest, and who treats me like he adores me.

That's what I want.

This kind of man.

Or, really, *this* man.

The man I wanted once upon a time when I was younger.

The one I'm about to have now.

Maybe this is why I waited. He was always the one I wanted.

But I can't get ahead of myself. I'm not looking for strings, and he's not either.

This can't go anywhere. Just enjoy it for tonight.

I am so damn ready to enjoy every second of him tonight.

Once the condom is on, Shane settles between my legs, meeting my eyes. "Still good?"

"So good," I say, parting my legs farther.

A wild groan seems to be ripped from his throat. "You're so fucking pretty," he says, then rubs the head of his cock against me.

My body crackles, sparking with lust. I arch against him, needing more.

"I want you," I whisper. I love saying those words, thrilled by speaking my dirty mind to a willing and eager sex accomplice at last.

Tingles race down my chest, and a new awareness hits me.

I love telling him what I want in bed.

Him. His cock. Our intimacy.

I meant it when I said I'm not innocent.

I have a sexual heart and mind, and I'm putting them to use tonight.

When he pushes in, my breath comes in a sharp gasp, and I tense from the intrusion.

"Okay?"

I nod. "Yes."

He sinks in more, and I wince.

"I can stop, love. Do you want me to stop?"

Narrowing my eyes, I growl. "Don't you dare."

A soft laugh comes from the man. He's braced on his

arms, his big hands pressed into the mattress by my sides. I slide my palms up his arms, traveling along his muscles as I breathe again, in, out, then deeper.

Let myself relax.

I'm ready.

"More," I say, urging him on.

And he gives.

Oh hell, does he ever.

He sinks all the way in.

I squeeze my eyes shut, adjusting, shifting, trying to relax into this foreign but almost fantastic sensation.

"Talk to me, love," he whispers.

Does he even know he says that in the heat of the moment? *Love?* Is he aware of what it does to my heart? It does things that Mr. Right Now shouldn't do for me.

It makes my heart sing.

The temporary pain washes away, and I linger in the goodness of *this*, in the rightness of him, in the truly fantastic sensation he's bringing me.

In this unexpected night of reconnection with my teenage boyfriend.

The guy I nearly fell in love with seven years ago.

I gaze up at him, our eyes locking, our bodies tangling. He looks at me like he cherishes me already, and surely it's the endorphins talking, but I like what they have to say. "Show me the joys of fucking and making love," I whisper.

"Both. I'll show you both," he says in a bedroom promise that sends sparks flying across my skin.

I let him know how joyfully I want it as I wrap my

legs around his firm ass, curl my hands over his shoulders, and move with my brand-new lover.

My one-and-only lover.

We find a rhythm, a sexy, indulgent pace that lights me up everywhere.

That's hotter than my fantasies.

More electric than any solo ride with a fourteen-speed vibe.

He hits me just right, his throbbing length sliding over my clit as he pumps and thrusts. He swivels his hips just so, and the languid, sexy move sends a current through my whole body.

Down my spine, all the way to my toes.

Dear God, my toes are actually curling, my body is melting, and pleasure coils in my belly.

Soon, I'm on the cusp of another orgasm. I can feel it just out of reach. It's almost there, on the horizon.

And I don't want to lose it, don't want to miss the chance to come again.

So I slide a hand between my legs and help myself along.

"Yes, fucking yes. That's so damn sexy," he says, encouraging me. "Play with yourself."

Don't need to tell me that twice. I'm there, rubbing and chasing my bliss as the guy who got away drives me to the edge of pleasure.

"I missed you, Clem. Fucking missed you so much," he rasps out on a broken pant, and his words send me flying.

Right over the edge as I call out his name when I shatter.

He's there with me, thrusting and grunting, and then he stills, groaning for what feels like forever.

In his arms, I'm keenly aware of three things.

I love sex.

I love sex with him.

And I want more than tonight.

But I know that I can't have it.

9

CLEMENTINE

When I shut the front door the next morning, the clock cat's tail mocks me.

It says, *Time is running out.*

I try to tear my gaze away from its mockery as I unclip Magnus's leash, then set down the two cups I just snagged at the shop on the corner when I took my guy for a morning bathroom break. I also caught up with Erin on my walk, but I'm going to need more girlfriend time later, since she had quite a night.

Now, though, I want to enjoy the little time I have left with the man in my bed. After our epic nooky, he asked to stay the night. No idea if that's normal for deflowering, but I like it.

My pooch barks, and it sounds like he's asking, *Where's Shane?*

The answer comes a few seconds later when he strolls out of the bedroom, hair still sleep-rumpled, and looking like all of my morning sex fantasies.

My brain pops.

Neurons mix with hormones, and my libido practically purrs.

He runs a hand through his hair, leans against the doorway, and stretches, looking like sin and dessert all in one package—he's wearing jeans and nothing else.

I would like to lick the grooves of all his abs.

"Morning, love," he says, then yawns.

I die.

I just die.

There is nothing left of me but my desire.

"Hi," I say, and it comes out all strangled, since what I really want to say is *Oh my God, can we please screw again against the kitchen counter? Because holy hell, you look like every dirty Tumblr video ever.*

Magnus takes off, running to the man, yipping and dancing.

Shane laughs, then bends down. "Is this the doggie dance?"

Oh hell.

That's it.

The strings are starting to attach.

"I think he likes you," I say, a little wistful, since what I want to say is *He's not the only one.*

Shane scoops him up in his arms, pets his head, then peers at me. "I hope he's not the only one."

My heart. It jackhammers.

Not fair, not fair, not fair.

I grab the cup of tea, thrust it in his direction. "I got you English breakfast." I lift the other cup. "And a coffee. Black. No presumptions, but I didn't know which you liked. Me? I'm, like, blood-type O with caffeine. I'll take it in all forms. You pick."

"Tea. Like I said, you can take the boy out of England . . ." With my tiny dog in his arms, snuggled against his bare chest, he strides across the floor to the kitchen, then drops a kiss to my cheek. His breath is minty fresh, and I dance a virtual jig, since I love fresh breath in the morning.

Love it so much I want more of it.

I turn my face so I can catch his lips.

"Mmm," he murmurs, then kisses me soft and gentle —a tender morning kiss. But one that doesn't end. One that feels dangerously like foreplay. Like a prelude. He lingers on my lips, brushing barely-there kisses against me like he's seducing me with slow, tantalizing touches.

It's working, Shane. It's working.

I'm outrageously aroused already. I'd go through ten panty changes a day if he were mine.

What?

Mine?

That's not happening.

That's not on the table.

I find the will to break the kiss, and when we separate, a scratchy pink tongue licks my face.

Saved by the dog.

I reach for my pooch, then take my boy in my arms. "This is not helping."

"What's not helping?"

I wave at him. "You being all shirtless and holding my dog and kissing me. That's why I took him from you."

He grins wickedly. "Maybe I wasn't trying to be helpful. Maybe I was trying to get you back in bed."

"Well, it's working," I say with a laugh.

"Excellent." He lifts the tea, takes a drink. "That was thoughtful of you. Thank you."

I shrug with a smile. "I can be thoughtful."

"I know," he says, and then just gazes at me, his lips curving into a grin.

And I can't look away. I don't want to do anything but stare stupidly back at his face.

My stomach flips. It handsprings.

And I wish this weren't ending.

I put my dog on the floor, trying desperately to break the spell of last night and this morning. I grab my coffee and knock some back. "So, you leave for spring training soon?"

He jerks his gaze to the cat clock. "Yes, in about eight hours."

I blink. "Oh. Do you need to go?"

He takes another drink, then sets down the tea. "Not yet. I have time."

I take one more fueling drink of coffee, then I put it down.

And I crash into him. We kiss madly. Desperately. In a collision of lips and teeth and bodies.

He reads my wants, senses my needs, but still, he asks, "Are you sure?"

"Do you mean, can I handle your monster cock again?"

Shaking his head, he laughs. "Just making sure you feel good."

"I feel great," I say, and in a minute, I'm up on the counter, skirt hiked up, panties gone, and legs spread.

He finds a condom in his wallet, then shoves down his jeans to his thighs and slides on the protection.

Seconds later, he's in me, and I'm a little bit tender from last night, but I don't care.

I want him again, just like this. Fucking me, taking me, having me.

And it's like a dream.

Only better, so much better. Because it's all real as we moan and rock and murmur.

And with our bodies speaking the same language, my mind gets ahead of me. Picturing him and us, and third times and fourth times. Then my mouth takes over. "I want this again. Want you again," I plead.

With a deep thrust, he groans, eyes meeting mine. "Want you again, too, love. Want you so much."

That's all it takes. Soon, we're both breathless and gasping, coming together, reaching for each other.

After, I grab him harder, hold him closer, and he does the same to me. Stroking my hair, whispering in my ear. "I'm so glad I ran into you," he murmurs, then like the moment has gotten the better of him, too, he says, "I'm going to miss you. I swear I'll miss you more than I want to."

I can hear what he's not saying.

Don't break my heart.

10

SHANE

I don't want to leave her, so I stretch out the hours I have. We go for a walk in her neighborhood, taking turns holding the dog's leash.

We catch up on her dog training, and she tells me about her clients, the challenges, and the victories. She asks me about my job, too, how it feels to have been traded so many times already.

"I suppose it might make someone feel unwanted," I joke.

She swats me playfully. "The opposite, silly. You're very wanted."

I kiss her cheek as we reach the corner. "Yes, seems that way. And I like it."

We're talking about baseball and also *not* talking about baseball.

As we wander along Polk Street, the world's fastest small dog leading the way, I ask about her family. "Mom and Dad are still grotesquely happy. My sister too. They truly set such a bad example for everyone," she deadpans.

"The worst," I echo.

"And your family?"

"Same, same. Dad is taking Mum to the Galápagos Islands right now. She loves to travel, so they're spending loads of time just gallivanting."

"Gallivanting. I feel like those are life goals," she says, then she startles at the sound of a beep. "Oh, that must be Erin again. She had an interesting night."

I lift a brow in question as she takes out her phone from her pocket, swipes open the screen, then smiles. "I'll answer it later," she says as she tucks it away again. "But I think it's safe to say someone has a crush."

"Erin, you mean?" I ask.

She knits her brow. "Who else would I mean?"

I laugh, a little embarrassed, almost like I've been caught red-handed.

I meant me.

Ah, hell.

I'm leaving in a few hours. No point truly being so guarded. It's not as if she can break my heart when I'm gone. "Well, it seems I have one too."

Her green eyes twinkle with delight. Maybe something else too. Something deeper? Perhaps hope?

She reaches for my hand and threads her fingers through mine. "Join the club."

* * *

We grab lunch, then return to her place and her bed once more. After that, we shower together, and then I truly do have to go.

"You better not miss your flight. I want to cheer for the Dragons on Opening Day, but if their brand-new closer is in trouble for being late to spring training, I won't be able to," she says, wagging a finger.

I grab her finger, nibbling on it. "I have excellent timing," I say, then I glance at her fingernail. It's polished with silver, and a Papillon is painted on it. "You found a nail salon that can do dog designs," I say with a bit of wonder in my voice.

"Of course I did. You say that like I'd do anything else."

She is adorable, and naughty, and open, and kind, and far too risky for my heart.

"All right, stop distracting me. Now I truly have to leave," I say, but I'm not letting go of her either.

I give her one more kiss, and as my lips brush hers, images and ideas flash past me. Future days and nights. Possibilities.

But last night, we agreed to no strings.

Crush or not, she doesn't want something serious.

And I need to look out for myself.

That's why I don't ask for her number. It's why she doesn't ask for mine.

Instead, I tear myself away from her and say good-bye, then I leave to head to Arizona.

I'm leaving her for baseball once again.

11

CLEMENTINE

A week later

I'm tempted to flip the bird at the cat clock when I leave for class one morning a week later.

But it's not the inanimate cat's fault that I'm counting the hours.

And for what?

What am I counting down to?

"Ugh. I'm the worst," I tell Magnus as I say goodbye at the door.

His little floofy tail whips back and forth, his butterfly ears standing tall, cocked in curiosity.

"Why? Because I'm . . . well . . ." I flap a hand. "I'm all . . . just a mess."

I kneel in front of him, and he puts his little paws on my chest.

"I don't even know why," I answer his unasked question.

He licks my nose.

"Fine, fine," I huff, since he's wearing me down. "I guess I hoped . . . I dunno."

I can't even say it.

It's so silly.

Such a virgin thing to wish for, I'm sure.

"So typical of the virgin. Wanting more. Falling for the first guy, right?" I ask.

He jumps a few times, a sign he wants to be held. "You're such a love monster," I say with a laugh, sinking down to my butt and cuddling my dude. He rubs his head against my chest, then nuzzles my face. "Ravenous, I tell you. That's what you are."

But maybe I am too. I feel greedy. And wildly hungry. Like I haven't eaten for days, and I'm starving. For more affection, more kisses, more fucking, and more . . . time.

But I told him *no strings*.

I meant *no strings*.

At least, at the time I did.

I say goodbye to Magnus, pop in my earbuds, and listen to the original Broadway recording of *Fun Home* as I head to teach an agility class.

Usually show tunes cheer me up.

But this time, they aren't quite doing the trick.

* * *

Later that night, I go out with my friends to dinner. For one of the first times ever, I'm not *the cheery one*.

I'm in a bit of a funk, and Erin notices, pulling me

aside after sushi. "Are you okay? You're usually more . . . ebullient."

"Nice five-dollar word," I say approvingly.

"Please. That's a ten-dollar word. But seriously."

I sigh heavily. She knows the details. "It's silly. I just wish that maybe Shane and I could have another shot. That maybe he wanted to as well."

Her eyes are thoughtful, her tone kind. "Do you know for sure he doesn't?"

"He said that," I tell her, but that doesn't feel entirely true either.

His kisses said more. But it was his eyes, and the way he looked at me when he left that said so much—that said he'd missed me, that he already longed for me.

At least, that was how I read him.

12

SHANE

A couple weeks later

Some say spring training games don't matter. There's a lot of truth to that for the guys who've already made the roster.

My spot is guaranteed.

I'll be ready for Opening Day, should there be a victory to save.

But guarantee or not, my father taught me that every game matters. You play hard, you pitch well, and you give your all.

That's how he played during his career, and that's what he taught me when I was growing up in England and then later in the States.

You never know who's watching.

You never know who needs you on your team.

But you should also play well for you. If you don't, you become complacent.

That's why my spring training stats rock.

I refuse to accept less than my personal best.

It's how I was raised. It's who I am.

We've only just started playing games against other teams here in Arizona, but already I'm putting up strikeouts and saves. Just like I plan to do in the regular season.

These are the type of stats that'll impress the owner.

After I close out a game with three strikeouts in a row, I stride off the field.

Drew trots over to me from the backstop, tapping his glove to mine. "Nice save, Shakespeare," he says. "Or should I say, *fourth* nice save."

I shoot him a satisfied smile. "You should definitely say that."

That's a good thing. That's what my agent wanted. For me to focus on baseball, not romance. Though, admittedly, romance hasn't been far from my mind since that last night in San Francisco.

At night when I get in bed, I think of Clementine.

When I wake up, she's on my mind.

When I'm alone, I imagine her.

And I *miss* her.

Good thing I'm not alone too often.

I shake thoughts of her away, focus on the here and now. The game. My teammates.

The shortstop and second baseman—Declan Steele and Holden Kingsley—knock fists with me as they head to the dugout. "Keep that up during the regular season, Shakespeare," Declan says.

"Count on it," I say as we continue on to the locker room.

"Dude, you are the epitome of cool on the mound," Drew remarks. "I'm telling you, when I'm playing, I have no chill."

I laugh at his tell-it-like-it-is attitude. "Because you're the catcher. You're allowed to be full of emotion. I have to be ice."

Drew furrows his brow. "Why don't we call you Iceman, then?"

"Excellent question to ponder," I say.

"How about we ponder it over burgers?"

"I'm in."

That night, we head to the Cactus Club, meeting up with Sullivan from the Cougars.

"Well, well, well. If it isn't the comedy club crew," Sullivan jokes as we join him at the bar. "That was a helluva night."

He's reminiscing about one night out from a few weeks ago?

Interesting. What was so special about that one time?

I arch a questioning brow. "I take it you're not simply talking about the comic?"

He shakes his head. "Nope."

Drew stares at him, then waggles his fingers. "Spill."

Sullivan shakes his head, taking a drink of his beer. "Not my story to tell, but suffice to say, I can't wait to get back to San Francisco." He lifts his hand, crossing his fingers. "That's all I'll say."

"Well, you're fun," Drew deadpans. "I can't wait to

get back to the city either, but at least I told you assholes why."

"You did, and you're so bloody adorable, all heart aflutter and whatnot," I say, teasing him.

He scoffs. "You're one to talk. You've been moony-eyed since that night too. I'm pretty sure your high school sweetheart is more than just some rando."

I tilt my head. Scratch my jaw. "I didn't tell you she was my high school sweetheart."

Drew cracks up, shaking his head. "I know. But I have sources."

"And what do your sources tell you?" I ask, and that piques my interest. "Are you talking about Clementine's friends?"

He shakes his head in slo-mo. "I'm telling you nothing. But you might want to check yourself later and figure out why you're so . . . *not chill* at the mere mention of her."

I heave a sigh, then order a beer, ignoring his remark.

He doesn't ask again, but as Drew and Sullivan chat about their favorite spots in San Francisco, then debate dream cars before arguing over whether the beach or the mountains is a better spot for a vacation, my mind drifts back in time once again.

To that night with her.

Images flash before my eyes.

Enticing, delicious ones.

But sweet ones too.

Laughing, teasing, talking.

Most of all, how she opened up to me.

How I opened up to her.

Then, I skip forward, imagining future days. What would they look like?

Would they be better with her in them?

I'm not the most open guy with my teammates, preferring to keep things light. But Drew seems more upbeat than I've seen him before, so maybe there's room to crack open this conversation.

Clearing my throat, I toss out my contribution to the bar debate. "Do you think romance and baseball can ever work?"

Sullivan laughs to himself.

Drew whistles.

"What does that mean?" I ask.

Sullivan arches a brow. "Dude, look around at your team and ask yourself that question." He rattles off the names of my Dragons teammates who've fallen in love lately.

Holden, Declan.

Then he gestures to himself. "My team too. All the guys are falling hard. Crosby. Chance. Grant."

Drew taps his chest, weighing in. "And so is *this* guy on your team too. In fact, I need to get back to my room for a little FaceTime date. So I'd say the answer is yes."

I wish I knew for sure if the answer was *yes* for me.

13

CLEMENTINE

I flop onto a black-and-white-striped couch in The Spotted Zebra a few nights later, checking the time on my phone.

My friends should be here soon, but Sierra—the bar owner—swings by, drops down next to me, and squeezes my shoulder.

"Do I need to dangle cupcakes in front of you to bring you to your Clementine senses?"

I pout at my friend. "It's that obvious?"

She rolls her eyes. "Normally, you're the happiest camper in the land. You ride in on your Pegasus," she says, rocking her head and making a *clip-clop* sound like she's on a horse. "And you fire rainbows from your dog-decorated fingers and sing to chipmunks."

"I am not a Disney princess," I say, insisting.

"Oh yes, you are!"

I turn to see Nova sashay in, all tall and leathery—well, she's wearing leather. She's not wrinkly. She's in a leather skirt and a leather vest, and the whole look is sex-ay.

"Badass babe! Whoa! Is it Leather Day?"

Nova casts me a *don't be silly* face. "Vegan here. I don't wear real leather. This is fake. It's made from tires or something," she says, gesturing to her outfit.

"Well, you look hot in tires or something," I say, as Erin and Frankie follow her in and join her on the couch across from mine. "And I'm not a princess."

Erin chuckles under her breath, her brown hair spilling across her face.

I kick her playfully. "I'm not." Then I peer at her. "Also, you look . . . happier."

She grins, wide and satisfied. "I am." Erin beckons us closer, then gives us the inside scoop on what she's been up to.

I'm kinda floored by her plans, yet they also make perfect sense. And I'll support her, of course, as she takes this chance.

I squeeze her knee. "I'm happy for you."

"Speaking of happy . . ." Sierra lets the sentence hang deliberately open before she casts a glance back to the bar. "I need to return to serving all my happy customers, so can you all tell Ms. Happy Till She's Not about our new plan for her?"

I let my jaw fall open in mock annoyance as Sierra takes off for the bar.

I turn to the others. "What have you been up to?"

Frankie smiles, pushing her glasses up her nose. "Sometimes you have to take a chance. Especially when you want something."

Erin nods a few times too. "You do, friend. You really do."

Nova crosses one leg over the other. "Putting yourself out there can mean more than just dating again. It can mean putting yourself out there for *one* person," she says, and my throat tightens.

Emotions arise in me, a slew of them. Missing Shane, wanting Shane, but also loving these ladies for knowing me so well. "I'm like cellophane. You can see right through me," I say, a knot of feelings tightening in my chest.

"Like the song from *Chicago*," Frankie adds, then pats my knee.

"Yes, you get me," I say, my voice shaky.

But why? Why am I so emotional? Oh, maybe because I have amazing friends who want the best for me?

"I want to talk to him again. To see him again," I confess, blurting out my true, messy heart.

"We thought as much," Erin says with a grin.

"But I don't even have his number. We didn't exchange numbers. We just said goodbye, agreeing it was for the best," I say, practically pleading to the universe to help me.

Erin barks out a laugh. "Friend, I got you. Gimme your phone. I tracked it down for you, so I'll enter it."

As my heart races—with hope—I hand her my phone. Thrilled that she went hunting. More thrilled that she *knew* I needed it. Knew I wanted it.

She enters his info, then hands the device back to me.

I crack up as I read the name she's typed in.

The Deflowerer.

Later, I open my phone to send him a text. But I startle when I see one from him.

14

SHANE

An hour earlier

Another day, another save.

Drew high-fives me in the locker room after a game against the Minotaurs. "You're the secret weapon," he calls out.

Bemused, I shake my head. "I'm just one piece of the puzzle."

"The missing piece," Holden shouts, then claps me on the back. "By the way, it is good to be reunited with you."

"Same to you," I say, since we played together on the Bandits before the team's owners unloaded a ton of players a few years ago.

"And we are going to have an epic Opening Day. The goal, gentleman?" he booms, speaking to the whole team now in the locker room.

The guys turn around and quiet down, no doubt thanks to Holden's commanding presence.

"The goal," he repeats, then claps my shoulder, "is to get this man on the mound every goddamn game. If we see Shakespeare coming in from the bullpen, it's a damn good day."

"Truer words," Declan seconds, leading a round of clapping.

They're not wrong.

I only show up if we're winning. If we need to close out a victory. "I hope to make many, many appearances," I say, and I long to show all these guys what I can do.

I also want to live up to my father's legacy.

I want to win the owner's trust.

And I want to enter arbitration in a great spot.

But as I leave the locker room that afternoon, my thoughts drift once again.

To Opening Day.

To something else I want.

To romance *and* baseball.

To one woman.

She hasn't left my mind since I've been here in Arizona. I'm not sure I want to play the whole season possessed by the idea of her. It seems that whether we're dating or not, my mind is on her—so why not try to play it another way?

With her in my life.

All the way in it.

As I leave, I call Drew aside. "That person you've been FaceTiming with? Think you can call in a favor, mate?"

"Name it."

"Can you slip me Clementine's number?"

He thumps me on the arm. "You dog. I fucking can. Look at you. Guess you're not just ice. You've got fire in there too."

I laugh.

Perhaps he's right.

Or maybe I just miss the woman far too much to deny these feelings any longer.

I suppose the heart is like that.

It wants what it wants.

And I want her.

No matter the risk.

15

From the Texts of Shane and Clementine

That night

Shane: Hello, love. I can't stop thinking about you. You're literally in my thoughts all the time. You're so much more than a crush.

Clementine: I SOUND LIKE A COPYCAT, BUT SAME, SAME, SAME. YOU ARE SO MUCH MORE THAN A CRUSH TOO!

Shane: Well, then, would you like to come to Opening Day when I return to San Francisco? And by come to Opening Day, I mean, would you like to be there in the stands as my date? Because the night before I want to take you to "adult prom." Go ahead, ask me what adult prom is.

Clementine: I'll bite. What's adult prom? Also, hi!!! I can't stop thinking about you either—just had to say that again.

Shane: Thank fuck for that. God, my head is full of you. I've replayed that night about ten million times. All of it.

Clementine: Twenty million for me.

Shane: Show-off.

Clementine: I know. Now tell me!

Shane: Adult prom will be held this year at the former site of the Carter Club. Aka the Luxe Hotel. Just you and me. I'd love to take you there, spend the night with you, and keep lavishing on you all the joys of fucking and making love.

Clementine: Adult prom sounds like the best thing ever! I say yes.

Shane: I can't wait to see you again and sweep you into my arms.

EPILOGUE

Clementine

Adult Prom

There's a knock on my door.

Magnus barks.

I run to the door, hopped up on jet fuel, driven by desire.

I swing it open and beam.

Then melt.

Then soar when Shane steps inside, hauls me against him, and kisses the breath out of me.

It's a passionate, soul-deep kiss, full of fire and longing.

And promise too.

It's a kiss that says, *I missed you so fucking much.*

And I kiss him back the same way.

When we come up for air, he tugs me close and runs a hand along my cheek. "I'm not letting you get away this time. Screw circumstance. You're not becoming an ex. You're mine. Say you're mine. I want you to be mine."

I laugh, bursting with joy and emotion as Magnus jumps at our feet. "I'm yours. You're not Mr. Right Now. I'm pretty sure you're Mr. Right." Then my hand flies to my mouth.

Shoot.

Did I say that aloud?

Will that scare him away?

But he drags me closer, brushes another kiss to my lips, then says, "Good. That's who I want to be to you. Your Mr. Right."

Goodbye, Queen of Terrible Dates.

I'm the queen of my own romance story, and I'm writing it with this guy—the guy I'm not letting get away.

I say goodbye to my pup, then we leave, head to the Luxe Hotel, and slow dance in the corner of the bar.

"Better than prom," he says.

"Big fan of adult prom," I say.

"Want to know what I like best?"

"Of course I do."

He roams a hand up my back, keeping his gaze locked on mine. "That I'm falling for you."

My heart sails away. "I'm falling so hard for you."

Then he takes me to a room and makes love to me.

And it's even better than the first time.

And the second time.

The third too.

Sheesh, we had a lot of sex that night.

But I really, really like sex with him.

Wait. Nope.

I love it.

Pretty sure I love him too.

But I also love my dog, so when I get up at six to go home and let him out, I whisper goodbye to my guy, figuring he'll stay in bed.

Instead, he joins me, and we take my dog for a walk together, then go back to sleep at my place.

Best adult prom ever.

* * *

That afternoon, I go to Opening Day and cheer him on. He saves the game and kisses me in the stands when it's finished.

And this is how we start over.

Remaking the past, shaping it into our brand-new present.

THE END

CAPTAIN ROMANCE

A VIRGIN SCORECARD NOVELLA

PROLOGUE

Sullivan

The October before that *Valentine's Day*

Women fascinate me.

Ever since I discovered the allure of curves, soft skin, and lush hair, I've been drawn to the fairer sex.

But it's not just the way women look. I'm wildly attracted to the minds of women too, and I desperately want to understand what makes women tick.

I've turned to many sources over the years in the pursuit of that knowledge. Psychology in college, then magazines and articles in my early twenties—anything to gain insight into my favorite subject.

I've devoured memoirs, podcasts, and novels too.

Romance novels, to be precise.

Just call me Captain Romance. I like to pop in my

earbuds on the San Francisco Cougars team plane and get lost in a world where the endings are always wins and no one strikes out looking in his last at bat.

I've learned a lot from these stories.

For the most part, women like a guy who listens. Who treats her like a queen. Who has rock-hard abs. And who can go all night long.

Check. Check. Check. And more check.

I've learned, too, that women are like snowflakes. No two are the same, so no matter how much research I do on my own, there's no substitute for hands-on study.

And I sure as hell would like to conduct some research with a smart, sexy, fantastic woman I see nearly every day.

Trouble is, she's the reporter who covers my team.

Which probably makes me off-limits to her.

So, I'll need some extra strategy to win her over.

1

SULLIVAN

True fact about being a Major League pitcher: the fans either love you or hate you, and the needle swings based on your latest game.

Deliver a shutout?

You're a god.

Serve up more than a couple runs?

You're washed up, over the hill, and ready for pasture.

That's especially true as a reliever. Your task is to either hold the other team down or to staunch the bleeding. You come in, get the guys out, send your team back to the dugout.

And you damn well better do it as quickly and as efficiently as possible.

It's a thankless job, so thank fuck it's no longer mine. After four seasons in the bullpen, I switched last year to the starting lineup, so I pitch every fifth game. I started and won game six in the World Series—a victory that gave us our first championship trophy.

I'd like to get us to the Fall Classic this season too.

But first, the divisionals.

I arrive at the ballpark for game five, warming up with Grant, my catcher, on the diamond. When we're done, I stride off the mound and meet him at home plate. He taps his glove against mine, as has been our ritual since the two of us came up together in the minors in Bakersfield, California, nearly six years ago.

"Let's make it a double," I say.

"That's the one and only plan," Grant says.

As we walk along the spongy grass, I do my best to avoid staring at the brunette babe on the third baseline.

Erin Madison, the spitfire of a reporter, knows her baseball history and isn't afraid to pitch a tough question, not even to our manager. She's talking to him right this second, likely lobbing a hardball at him.

She's so fearless that it's hot.

Ah, hell.

I steal a glance after all, cataloging her brown hair curling over her shoulders, her trim figure, and the intensity in her eyes as she ends the interview, nodding her thanks.

I'm stepping into the dugout when she catches my eye and calls out, "Hey, Sullivan. Got a second for your favorite network?"

"Run, Sully, run," Grant teases under his breath.

I roll my eyes at my catcher. "I do not run when she calls my name. I strut."

Waving me off, he laughs. "Keep telling yourself that."

I leave him behind and head along the third baseline

to the woman who revs my engine, and has for some time.

I flash a smile, wishing she were anyone but the beat reporter. Pretty sure it'd be a mess for her if she went on a date with an athlete she covered. Might look like she'd slept her way to insight, to team secrets, to answers.

Stop thinking about sleeping with her.

The thing is, I want to do more than take her to bed. I want to spend time with her. Get to know her more. *Talk.*

I meet her blue-eyed gaze and decide to have some fun. "Hey, Erin, how do you feel about our chances tonight?"

She smiles, laughing lightly. "Good, as always, but why don't you let me ask the questions?"

Maybe I'm just a hopeful guy, but I'm hearing some flirting in her voice too.

I'll take what I can get.

I give an easy shrug. "Just like to keep you on your toes," I say, my gaze straying down to her shoes—red ballet flats.

"Which is what you'll aim to do against the Texas Scoundrels tonight. Keep them on their toes. But their bats have been on fire lately," she segues, then asks some questions about expectations for the game.

I answer them all, every damn one.

"So, what's the one key thing the Cougars must do to pull off back-to-back World Series victories?" That's been the theme of every interview for the Cougars in this postseason. Can we make it all the way again? "Is that on your mind a lot, Sullivan?"

"Yes. But you can only play one game at a time. So that's what I focus on—the game I'm in now."

She nods, seeming satisfied with that answer as she clicks off her camera. When she lowers her mic, she whispers, "Good luck tonight. I'll be rooting for you."

Not gonna lie. Those words make my chest swell with pride. They send a sizzle over my skin. I sure do like that she's a closet fan of the team too.

I give her my best crooked grin. "I'll keep your fangirl secret safe," I whisper.

"Yes, please do that," she says.

Sure, I want to do well for her, but I want to do well for the fans, the team, and my family too. All those factors fuel me that night, and I shut down the Scoundrels for the first four innings, then allow them one run before shutting them down again through the eighth.

Our closing pitcher comes in and seals the victory, so the Cougars are tied up in the divisionals against the Scoundrels. Tomorrow night, we can advance to the championship series if we win, and as we leave the field, I'm sure I see a look of relief in a certain sports reporter's eyes.

* * *

Trouble is, the next night, our starting pitcher for game six struggles on the mound, and all our relievers can do is stop the bleeding. We still lose by a disgusting nine runs. Our chances to advance die right alongside our repeat World Series hopes.

None of the Cougars are happy when the game ends. I trudge into the locker room, shower, and grab my phone and wallet. I say my goodbyes to the guys and take off.

As I head toward the ballpark's exit, I weigh my options for taking my mind off our shitty end to the baseball year. Then I spot Erin up ahead in the corridor, her backpack sliding down her shoulder, her tripod slipping out of her arms.

I bolt over. "Let me help you."

She waves me off, shrugging the bag back onto her shoulder. "I'm used to doing it by myself."

"But I don't mind," I insist, reaching for the tripod to see if she'll let me help. "I can definitely walk you to your car."

She seems to consider that for a moment, then nods, smiling at me. "I won't fight you on this one."

She lets me have the unruly tripod, and I rest it on my shoulder like a bat. "Then I am at your service," I say.

And as we head toward her car, I can't help but wish I could be at her service in other ways.

But maybe spending more time with her off the field will help convince her that I am a risk worth taking.

2

ERIN

I'm pretty self-sufficient.

I always carry my own gear. I've never had a camera guy. Don't need one. That's how it goes now with sports reporting.

You've got to learn to do it all on your own.

I've been doing it for the last four years, covering baseball in this city since I graduated from college with a journalism degree.

But I definitely don't mind a little help from number twelve on the Cougars.

Fine, fine, it doesn't hurt that Sullivan Fitzgerald is mega easy on the eyes. Sandy-brown hair, warm brown eyes, all California beachgoing charm, with sun-kissed skin and a smile for days.

But Sullivan's so much more than a looker.

The outgoing, curious, open-minded pitcher has always seemed interested in talking.

Talking *to me*.

Interviews with him last longer than they do with

other guys. We chat about motivation, emotion, feelings. And every time I've run into him at an event, we wind up going down the rabbit hole of baseball history.

He's such a student of the game, and so am I.

Same goes for the city we love. Sometimes when I turn off the mic, we keep going, sharing quirky observations about the city by the bay.

He's . . . a little addictive.

As we exit the ballpark, I jump at the chance to chat with him some more. He always seems to dig the deeper questions, and I relish the opportunity to understand a player beyond the PR-friendly answers.

I want to understand the man after a game like tonight's.

I turn to face him, our gazes connecting under the lights in the parking lot. "No cameras. This is totally off the record. But . . . how are you truly feeling this evening?"

He lifts one brow high. "Is this where you want me to tell you how utterly heartbroken I am?"

Funny, but he doesn't sound devastated. Perhaps he's covering it up, but he sounds . . . balanced. "Sometimes you seem like you want to talk about it," I say, hoping I'm reading him right.

He slows his pace. "Actually, I'm glad you asked."

"Whew," I breathe out hard, teasing a little, but mostly making sure I didn't cross a line. "Thought you were going to recommend a banishment from the press room."

He scoffs, shaking his head. "Never. Hardly anyone

ever asks something that actually digs a little deeper into feelings."

That's interesting, but maybe this question is also an opportunity to feed a certain restless hunger I've been experiencing lately. I'm not sure what it is, or where it's coming from, but this last season, I've been wanting to dig deeper at work—to indulge in a five-course meal now and then, rather than living off the bite-size stories I have to churn out daily.

"I truly want to know," I tell Sullivan. His eyes swing to mine like he's measuring my answer in them, making sure I mean it. Many pro athletes, understandably, don't open up much with reporters. The media is often the enemy. Best to put him at ease. "I want to know for me though. Off the record. As . . . *friends*," I say, testing out that word. It feels right with him, like we've become amiable with each other this season.

His casual smile reassures me, or perhaps both of us, that we understand each other. "As friends, then, Erin, the answer is . . . of course I wish we'd won. I wanted it desperately. Always do. Every game. Every time I'm on the mound. It's a kind of madness and has been with me since I can remember. But a good madness, I like to think."

"The madness that motivates you to do the work?" I ask, following the thread.

"Exactly. To put in the hours every single day. The madness gives me focus." It comes out as a growl, straight from his heart. "I can feel it in my bones with every pitch. If I ever lost that feeling, it'd probably be a sign to quit."

"Don't quit," I tease.

"Ha. No worries there. I definitely felt that intensity when I pitched last night. Tonight, too, in the dugout. But it's not just about chalking up the W. I want the win for my team. I want to pull together for them and to play the sport as best I can." He takes a pause, dialing down the ferocity. "But the secret is, if I truly give everything I have, I can handle it when we *don't* win," he says as we walk down the next row in the lot.

I gobble up his words, savoring every morsel. "Giving it your all means you can live with whatever the outcome is."

"Yes. Exactly. When I've played my absolute best, I can leave the emotions behind and move on. That's why I feel fine. Though, truth be told," he says, letting his eyes take a quick tour of my frame before coming up to meet mine, "I also feel pretty good right this second."

Another spark ignites inside me from his sultry gaze. But this one fans my body rather than my mind.

"Glad you feel good," I say, though I'm not sure what to do with his flirtiness. I like it so very much, yet it's risky.

I collect myself, taking a deep breath, then we continue to my car. "So, if you had won tonight, you'd be celebrating with the team. When you don't win, what happens? Do you go home in a funk?"

Asking questions is easier than figuring out the risk of flirting with a player I cover.

He levels a steely stare my way, all over-the-top. "Are you ready for the scoop?"

I laugh. "So ready."

"And we're off the record?" he confirms as we reach my car.

"I pinky swear." I lift my little finger, and he sets down the tripod to wrap his around mine, making me laugh. But my laughter stops quickly as a tingle has the audacity to slide down my chest, just from our fingers touching.

What the hell, body? Pinky swears aren't supposed to feel this good.

Yes, Sullivan's attractive.

Yes, I've always liked talking to him.

But I'm not supposed to feel anything remotely sparky for a man I report on for a living.

We unwrap our fingers, and I try to focus on talking rather than on feeling. "Are you going to tell me now?"

"I like to walk through the city. To wander around San Francisco or wherever I am."

That's a fantastic image. The pro athlete becomes the nomad at night. "You walk it off," I say, letting that little detail about him whirl around my brain. "That sounds cathartic."

"It actually helps me stay kind of balanced about the good madness."

"And it's why you can handle things when you don't win. You have your strategies." I nod my understanding, then click open the trunk to stow my gear. When I'm done, I turn back to him. "So, will you walk tonight?"

"I will," he says as the stars flicker in the night sky. "Do you want to join me?"

Something about his invitation feels a little risky. But it's only risky if I cross a line.

And I won't. I simply won't. A walk is just a walk.

I'm enjoying this new insight into players—into *him* —so why shouldn't I head out into this city we both love and educate myself some more?

"I would love to," I reply.

We leave my car behind and go.

3

SULLIVAN

This is my chance—time with this intriguing woman. A chance to get to know my friend a little better.

I even have a hunch what she might like.

"First stop. North Beach."

That's what I tell Erin when we exit the parking lot, strolling in front of the ballpark, the crowds having thinned out for the night.

With a curve on her lips, she arches a brow. "North Beach? Let me guess. You're a Joe DiMaggio fan? Is that why we're heading there?"

Ah, she is good. The one-time Yankees star did hail from that neighborhood. "Yes, but I'm not taking you to his usual stomping grounds." I know all of them, from the church where he married his first wife to the ballparks he sponsored over the years. But Erin's obsessed with the city's history, and a few weeks ago at a charity event, she mentioned she'd never seen some of the murals in the North Beach neighborhood. That's where I want to take her tonight, since, well, I'm hoping she likes a guy who listens. "I have something else in mind. How do you feel about surprises?"

With a twinkle in her blue eyes, she nods. "I'm pretty good with them. I feel like my entire job is a surprise. So, whatever you have in mind, Mister Walk It Off, I am good with it," she says, adding a bring-it-on lift of her chin.

Oh man, that doesn't help alleviate my crush on her. Her can-do attitude fans the flames.

It's another thing I like about her. She's open-minded and spontaneous—she rolls with the punches.

Maybe tonight will surprise us both.

Perhaps the travels through the city will help her see what we have in common. That I'm a guy worth considering, even if I'm a risk for her.

I could be a risk worth taking. I'm not interested in playing the field. I'm interested in finding the right woman for me.

Someone who wants the same things I do—passion, connection, intimacy.

I swear, there's something flickering between us, and I want to convince her to take a chance with me.

"And to answer your question, I'm obviously a fan of Joe DiMaggio, but I'm taking you someplace else in North Beach. Someplace completely unrelated to baseball."

"Well, I'm excited for your tour. And did you know DiMaggio is one of what I call the Originals?" she asks, tossing that out there with a sassy wink—one that says she wants to play the game of Stump Each Other.

Since I'm a competitive guy, I'm down for that. "I'll

bite. By Originals, do you mean he was the first hundred-thousand-dollar man?" The New York Yankee was the first baseball player to earn that milestone salary back in 1949.

She whistles in appreciation as we turn the corner, heading to the vibrant nearby hood. "I'm duly impressed. But that's not what I mean," she says. "By Originals, I mean he was one of the first pro athletes to buy a home for his parents. In 1939, he bought them a house in the Marina."

"Ah, was he the one who started that trend?" I ask. It has kind of become a thing in professional sports. Lots of guys buy their parents a new home when they hit certain milestones.

"Maybe he was. He bought it for them after he won his fourth World Series," she says, rattling off details about DiMaggio's gift to his parents.

Hmm. Interesting that Erin sounds so enthused about this act of generosity. Maybe this is a clue to her heart.

"You've got to give back. I actually paid off the mortgage for my parents in San Diego a couple of years ago." I might as well let her know I'm a generous guy too. Maybe that'll help smooth my way past this sorta work, sorta friendship zone.

As we walk through the San Francisco night, she beams at me. "How did they react? I want all the details," she says, rubbing her palms together.

My mind flashes back to that day, the memory flickering in Technicolor. "When I landed my first big contract after my third year, I went home to San Diego in the off-season. The first day I was there, I headed to the bank. My financial advisor worked out all the details behind the scenes to pay off the mortgage with the company that held it for the bank. So, I just went in and signed and paid . . . then I took them out to dinner to their favorite Italian restaurant. I had a gift inside a box with a ribbon around it. I took it out over cannoli."

Under the streetlamps, her irises sparkle, like every detail feeds her appetite for more. "And then what?"

I recall the curious look in their eyes, my pride that I'd been able to do this for them—the sense of accomplishment. "I handed them the box. Mom opened it with nervous but eager fingers and found the title to the house in it. I told them they owned their home free and clear. And then I said thank you," I say, a hitch in my own voice at the memory. "Mom got up from the table and threw her arms around me, wrapping me in the biggest hug. She cried. Dad did too."

Erin flings her hand to her heart. "That's beautiful," she says, caught up in the emotion too. "Was it something you'd always wanted to do?"

"It was a dream, but a far-off one that I wasn't sure was possible. At first, when I was in the minors, I just wanted to make it to the show. And I wasn't even sure if I'd make the roster my first spring training in Arizona. I definitely had some wobbly games."

"Everyone does though. That's normal."

"True, but you're only allowed so many." I shake my head, relieved that I worked past mine. "I didn't do it alone. Grant helped a ton. When I had a couple bad games, he did extra practice with me, then rounded up some of the other guys the next morning too. Crosby was there. Declan too, when he played for us. They helped me get my feet back under me . . . and the rest is history."

"See? These are the kinds of stories I want to tell someday. It's beyond the stats. It's a great tale of teamwork."

I nudge her arm with my elbow. "And I thought this night was off the record. Now I learn you're just trying to get my best stories out of me," I tease as we near Columbus Avenue, the street that cuts through the heart of North Beach.

She gives me a deliberately evil grin. "Are there more? Gimme, gimme, gimme."

I lean my head back, laughing. "Apparently, all you have to do is take me for a walk and I spill my secrets."

"I want all your secrets, Sullivan," she says. "We'll walk all night long if that's what it takes."

Is that a hint of flirt in her voice?

I don't have time to decide. "So, your parents. The house," she prompts. "Was it a dream of yours?"

I scrub a hand along my nape, thinking back. "It was definitely my goal to make their lives easier. My parents worked hard when I was growing up, running a nonprofit that provided counseling services for those who couldn't afford it, and I knew I could make a difference for them. Hell, they made a difference for me. They took me to all my games, all my practices. My mom sat in the bleachers with her computer, reviewing programs and donations during my games. So, it was fitting that I should give back to them."

Erin sighs happily and shoots me a swoony smile. "You're too sweet." She takes a deep breath. "Now, moment of truth. Did you cry too, when you gave them the title?"

A fair question, and I wouldn't be ashamed if I had. But telling the truth has gotten me this far with Erin—spending more time with her, out of the pressroom, away from the field. Best to stick with that.

"I'm not a crier," I say. "Unless my football team loses. That shit makes me sad. And I'm sad a lot because I'm from San Diego. So now I root for the Hawks."

"Smart move, switching to a team that wins," she says.

I tap my temple. "Brilliant, I know." Then, I shrug. "Honestly, I'm not a crier. Probably because I'm in my head most of the time."

She hums, like she's processing that tidbit. "You know, that makes a lot of sense. You need to be more cerebral than emotional to do your job."

We turn onto Columbus, walking past a café that reeks of garlic and pesto. "You've hit the nail on the head," I say, appreciating the way she understands my role on the mound.

"That's probably why you were able to handle a starting pitcher change. Some of the best guys in the game are those who are able to separate their game from their emotions. Sometimes you just need to be both in your mind and your body but not really in your heart."

"Yes. There's a time and a place for emotions on a baseball field," I agree. "But I imagine it's the same for you as a reporter. If you were covering a player who was injured, for instance."

Her eyes widen, and she grabs my arm like a lifeline. "Like earlier this year when Manuel Rosa broke his leg during a game," she says, mentioning the Storm Chasers center fielder.

I shudder at the memory. She does too.

But then my eyes drift down to her hand on my biceps. That feels pretty damn good, and I log new data in my Erin file—she's a toucher. She has an emotional side. She's full of energy. She can barely stop moving.

Damn it. She's so fucking right for me.

She doesn't let go of my arm as she jumps back to the topic. "Confession: I kind of am a crier. I went home that night Rosa was hurt, and I was heartbroken for him. It just looked so bad. I interviewed him a few days later, and he was devastated."

A pang lodges in my chest. I'm lucky I haven't had that kind of injury. "I can't imagine. Hell, I don't want to imagine."

I turn from that distressing idea, shifting the tone to something lighter. "My turn with the questions, Miss Reporter Who Never Stops Asking Questions." I grab an imaginary mic and hold it in front of her as we walk. "You heard my story about my parents. Give me one of yours."

"Fine, fine," she says with a huff. Then she straightens her shoulders, like she's getting all serious. "Let's see. I didn't buy them a house. But I do give them cute thank-you cards when a story of mine goes viral."

I gesture for her to go on. "More. Details. Now."

"So demanding," she says, bumping her shoulder to mine—though it's more like her shoulder to my biceps. "I send them cards that my friend Frankie makes. She's a florist, but the cards are her side hustle. They're all fruit themed—like an illustration of bananas winking, and it says, *Thanks a bunch.* Or a peach smiling, and it'll say, *I a-peach-i-ate you.*"

"Certifiably adorable," I say. "But we are not done, woman. Why do you thank them?"

She cracks up, then clears her throat. "They didn't want me to have any student debt, so they made sure when I went to college that it was completely paid for. I feel incredibly lucky, so I try to thank them by doing a great job. It kind of drives me every day, the fact that they worked so hard with that goal in mind."

My heart thumps stronger for her, filling up with more feelings, more interest. I'm both touched and a little saddened. It's awesome that she feels this way, and it reminds me what I'm up against in my pursuit of her. She loves her work fiercely, and she's motivated by her family. Yet her work—and my role in it—is our biggest obstacle.

It's also what I admire so much about her.

"You love what you do," I say, putting it plainly. The pure simplicity of it.

"Mostly," she says with a note of longing. "I want to do more with it though. I love telling stories—the kind I don't quite get to tell."

"What kind?"

She sighs deeply. "Stories that show the people behind the game. Or even just people in general.

Human interest stories about the city, about sports, about icons."

"You want to dive into what makes someone tick," I say.

She flashes a blinding smile. "Exactly. Don't get me wrong—I'm crazy about my work. Borderline obsessed. But I also think I could do more with it."

"Personally, I think that sounds perfect for you. This whole walk, you've been digging into me," I say, jamming my fist against my chest like I'm scooping out the insides.

"Aww, did it hurt?"

"Only a little bit."

"Will you survive?" she asks with exaggerated concern.

"It's highly debatable," I deadpan. Then I turn a touch more serious. "But I hope you can do the work you want someday. You'll be the best at that too. And I mean that."

"Thanks. That's what I want," she says. "To do my best."

She wants to be tops at her job. Can she, though, if she gets involved with me? Is that a line she can't cross?

There's only one way to know. I'm going to ask her.

Now.

Fucking now.

It's time.

I take a breath, bracing myself. "Hey, Erin. Would you ever—"

Her hand darts out, grabbing my arm and yanking me close.

She drops her voice to a whisper. "That's Hudson Tanner's limo over there."

I jerk my gaze toward the sleek black vehicle idling at the light. Hudson Tanner's the owner of my team.

"Don't look!" she hisses. "Rumor has it that if he runs into any of his players on the street, he will just talk and talk and talk about the last game. He likes to discuss everything that went wrong."

Yup. She heard right. "All too true. Grant said he got cornered by him once after a game. And since the last thing I want to do is shoot the shit with the owner about how our team belched up a victory tonight . . . there's only one solution."

I grab her hand and tug her down an alley.

We run like hell.

And this woman, holy fuck. She's got lungs and legs on her, keeping up a good clip till we're well out of view.

We slow our pace, stopping, panting from the unexpected sprint down—I scan our surroundings—Jack Kerouac Alley.

She runs a hand through her hair, catching her breath.

Damn, she looks good in the starlight.

So incredibly good that I'm dying to tell her that she's been the object of my daydreams for a while now.

Everything about the last hour has clarified what I want.

I want to pursue a relationship with Erin.

Starting tonight.

4

ERIN

The temptation is strong.

The desire to step over the line thrums in my chest, taunts my better judgment.

Kiss him.

I'm pretty good at reading people. It's part of the job —listening, paying attention. I've been doing that all night, and I know one thing. Players don't hang out with reporters this long. It's just not typical.

Men do. Men who are interested in women. And women who are interested in men do the same.

They go for late-night strolls. They hang out after midnight. They tempt fate.

I want Sullivan Fitzgerald. But can I truly take that kind of chance, dating an athlete? How would that look to my network? To the public? While I wouldn't be the first reporter to date a sports star, I'm not sure it's the best move at age twenty-five, still growing and learning.

I don't want future employers to say I dated my way up.

I don't want athletes on other teams to decline to talk to me.

And I'm not sure I'm ready to take the risk of this going wrong.

If a romance with Sullivan doesn't work out, it would be messy. I follow the team. I travel with the team. I'm the one covering their schedule, reporting on the trades, interviewing the players before and after games. It's exhausting and wonderful, energizing and tiring, and it's part of who I am.

Work is all-encompassing. Getting ahead is the focus.

But right now, my body is the focus, and my lust is the epicenter of me. It's telling me to get closer, maybe even a little closer still, and to ask for a kiss.

Because, my God, his lips.

They look so soft and pillowy and lush. Sullivan has a fantastic mouth, one I can't stop looking at, and deep brown eyes I could get lost in. Eyes that gaze at me like he wants to crowd me against the wall and kiss me deeply into the night.

He licks the corner of his lips, like that's why he pulled me into this alley—to kiss in the moonlight. I want to so badly. Want *him* so badly.

Sullivan swallows roughly. "Erin," he begins, all husky and sexy.

"Yes?" My voice feels like it's hanging on a thread of desire.

"This might sound . . . out of the blue," he says. That confidence he carries onto the mound is gone. He's pure vulnerability now, and it's so enticing. "I would love to take you out again."

Oh God.

There it is.

The ask.

My chest aches with longing.

"I want to. I truly do," I say, and for a spell, his eyes glimmer with excitement, with all sorts of possibilities. I have to squash those. I can't give in. Even though when I look at him, I can feel the sizzle, the connection, but the raw danger too.

Don't date an athlete on your beat.

In my four years as a reporter, I've followed that unwritten guideline faithfully. Hell, I've pretty much followed a no-dating guideline, though unintentionally.

I shove my hands into my pockets so I'm not tempted to grab him, to feel his big frame against mine.

I need to be careful, to remember my parents paying for my school, the opportunities I have in front of me. I shouldn't squander them because of this intense attraction.

"You do?" he asks, snagging on my last words. "Because I do, so much. I want to get to know you better. Spend time with you."

Dear God, he makes that sound amazing—the chance to pursue this attraction that's physical and mental and emotional.

Trouble is, I can't. "I want all that too, Sullivan. But it's too much of a risk to my career," I say, sounding desperate—feeling a little desperate too. "I'd have to disclose it at work with HR, and then I worry that players and management would talk about me and treat me differently."

And work truly is everything to me. It's why I haven't invested much energy in men before. Hell, it's why I'm still a virgin.

His shoulders sag for a moment, but his expression is resolute. He nods crisply. "I understand completely. I don't want that burden to fall on you."

I heave a sigh, wishing there were another option.

Wishing I could take this risk.

But this thing flickering between us is too new.

Too fragile.

"Thank you for understanding," I say, fixing on a smile to lighten the mood. "But I would truly like to be friends with you. I don't mean *let's just be friends*. I mean, I think you and I could actually be friends. Real friends."

My hands feel clammy. Nerves twist, waiting for his reaction to my offer.

Maybe he doesn't want friendship.

Maybe he'll move on right now, find another woman to pursue. Pickings aren't slim for a guy like him—a major leaguer with a fat contract, a ring, a heart of gold.

A face for movie posters.

I feel like I'm waiting an eternity for an answer. Maybe because this question feels as risky, in its own way, as saying I want to date you.

Because I'm saying, *I like you. Are you interested enough to just hang out with me?*

A second later, Sullivan smiles, a crooked grin that reaches his eyes. "I'm good with that, Erin," he says, and I breathe again, relieved and excited. "For what it's worth, I think it's ridiculous that society judges women so harshly and lets athletes get away with all kinds of shit. But how about this? Let me show you the murals I wanted to give you a tour of."

"How did you know . . ." I stop myself, remembering, and I grin. "I told you at the charity event."

He winks. "I listen, Erin. I definitely listen."

I do love a listener.

5

SULLIVAN

I've been friend-zoned.

Not my first choice, but not totally unexpected either.

I can handle it.

The friend zone is like coming into the seventh inning against a tough left-handed batter.

Sometimes you strike him out; sometimes he homers off you. But you take your chances.

This is an opportunity, so I seize it.

Under the streetlamps of this city, I take her on a walking tour of some of the newest murals in North Beach, showing her a recent addition in this alley that celebrates some of the city's Asian heritage with illustrations and inscriptions. She devours them, reciting the words, then we move to the wall of the Vesuvio Café, debating the poem written on the bricks and its closing line: *It's time for another martini.*

"Words to live by," I say.

"Definitely."

We check out a few more, and when the clock strikes two, my stomach growls.

She pats it, and oh, yes, I like her hand on my stomach. A lot. I wish she'd keep it there, yank up my shirt, trace my skin with her tongue.

Someday . . .

"Pancakes?" I ask.

"There is only ever one answer to that question," she says, and we find a twenty-four-hour diner and tuck into our meal.

When we're done, she lets out a yawn the size of a container ship.

"Bedtime for you," I say, then call a Lyft to take us back to the ballpark.

On the ride, she yawns again, her eyelids fluttering. "I should warn you—I'm a little bit in love with sleep."

That settles it. "I'm going to drive you home, then," I tell her.

"You don't have to," she says on another yawn.

But this isn't about obligation. "I want to," I insist, and with good reason. She looks ready to crash, and I don't want that to be literal.

When we reach her car in the lot, I hold out my hand for her keys. "Shotgun for you, Erin."

She raises her hands in surrender. "I won't protest."

I drive her home, then grab her gear and walk her to the front door of her building.

She perks up a bit, giving me a soft, wistful sigh. "Tonight was amazing."

I couldn't agree more. It was amazing and enlightening. It solidified what had been just speculation. There is something brewing between us, and I want a chance to prove I'm worth the risk.

But that starts with listening to her. Respecting her wants and wishes. Being friendly. "What are you doing next week? Since we're friends, I was thinking we could hang out as friends. Maybe check out some more hidden gems in the city?"

She smiles brightly. "I would love to do that."

I give her a chaste kiss on the cheek.

Well, sort of chaste. I do linger, inhaling the faint traces of coconut on her skin, maybe from her lotion.

I draw a long inhale, then whisper, "Good night."

She shivers, then steps back. "See you next week."

6

ERIN

The Off-Season

My heart shimmies as I read the text message from Sullivan the next Saturday morning.

Sullivan: Agree/disagree—you're never too old for a slide.

Erin: All the way agree.

Sullivan: I thought you might feel that way.

Erin: And why's that?

Sullivan: You've got a "Sure, I'll go skydiving" attitude.

Erin: Um, hate to break it to you, but I've never gone skydiving.

Sullivan: But I bet you'd consider it. I bet you've gone hang gliding, rock climbing, and white-water rafting.

Erin: Are you reading my high school journals? Yes, all three.

Sullivan: There. I'm right. Anyway, I'll pick you up at six p.m. tonight. A twilight *friend date*.

I settle into my couch, setting down my phone. He really meant it when he accepted my friend offer. He actually wants—*gasp*—to be friends. And I can't stop smiling as I work on a piece to pitch to my network.

When evening rolls around, I close my laptop, shower, put on makeup, and get ready to . . . well, ride on my ass down a slide.

Whatever he has in mind, I'm going to like it.

* * *

I don't mind his emerald-green McLaren.

Not one bit.

Especially since he blasts hip-hop music. "Loved this playlist when I was a rookie," he says. "Still do."

"Some things never change," I muse, then tap the dash. "Like good tunes."

As he cruises into the Noe Valley neighborhood, he offers a fist for knocking and I accept.

We're buddies, and I like it.

A few minutes later, we arrive at the Seward Street Slides, and he parks the car.

"Yes! I was hoping we were going adult sliding here," I say, pumping a fist.

"I even brought the cardboard," he says, grabbing the thick pieces of a box from the trunk.

"We're going down the butt ramp," I say.

"Warning—I might scream like a dude going down a slide."

I nod approvingly. "Points for not saying scream like a girl."

He scoffs. "As if I'd say that. Not a sexist pig, Erin."

I bump my shoulder to his. "I know, and I like it."

"Good. You should," he says, kind of sexy and rumbly. Or maybe that's just how everything he says sounds to me—like I want to take off my clothes and roll around in it.

Or I would, if we were something other than *just friends*.

We traipse through the park, heading to the slides— two long, steep concrete chutes down a hillside.

"A hidden gem in San Francisco," he says when we reach the top.

"You are such a San Francisco historian," I tell him. "And I'm into that."

"Had a feeling you might be."

I eye the slide, and a kernel of worry digs into my chest. "Are you even allowed to do this, contractually?"

He presses his finger to his lips. "Shhh. Keep my secret, Erin."

I pretend to zip my lips as he sets down a piece of cardboard. "Ladies first," he says.

"You want me to die first, clearly," I tease.

"Ha. More like I want you to have the first slide-gasm."

I can't resist. I step a little closer, giving him a smile. "Slide-gasm. Nice. Very nice."

His eyes darken for a few seconds, lingering on my lips. "There's more where that came from."

"I bet," I say, loving his flirt even though I know I shouldn't.

Instead of indulging in more of that temptation, I park my booty on the cardboard and fly.

I scream in glee.

Soon, I'm at the bottom, bouncing up, breathless and thrilled, but thinking quickly. Grabbing my phone from my front pocket, I turn on the camera and snap a shot of the starting pitcher as he careens down the slide, his face shining with joy in the twilight.

He hits the bottom, jumps up, and thrusts his arms in the air. "Slide-gasm for this guy," he says.

I lift a hand to high-five. We smack palms. "I felt it too," I say playfully, but I don't let go of his hand.

He doesn't let go either. Instead, he curls his fingers tighter, wrapping his hand around mine. My breath comes faster. My pulse surges.

And we stay like that for a few more seconds, our gazes caught.

I squeeze his hand. This is all I'll allow—this little touch after the fun we had.

He rubs his thumb along my wrist. "You liked it?" he asks.

"So much," I say, but I'm talking about him too.

* * *

A couple weeks later, I make a plan for the Filbert Steps.

I like climbs, and since Sullivan works his body for a living, he can handle it.

I tell him as much in our text.

Erin: Next friend date—all the stairs!

Sullivan: Bring it on.

Erin: You're known for your love of stairs. That's what your journals told me. Wink, wink.

Sullivan: They were right. There are no stairs I can't handle.

Erin: Same here.

Sullivan: Damn, woman, you do like to throw down.

Erin: Confession: I love stair workouts.

Sullivan: Confession: I. Do. Too.

We meet on a Sunday, tackling the long set of stairs up to Coit Tower. They're perfect for exercise, and maybe that'll take my mind off the kisses I can't have with Sullivan. It should help my focus on keeping my heart rate up.

We wind our way through the neighborhood, heading for the steps.

He takes the first step, then turns to me. "Hey, are we still off the record?"

I roll my eyes. "Dude, we've been off the record for a while."

"Good. Then I'll tell you officially I wasn't supposed to go adult sliding a couple weeks ago. It's against my contract," he whispers.

My mouth forms an O. "Just as I suspected. And you are so naughty."

"I'm an outlaw, Erin," he teases as we climb. "Good thing we're always off the record."

"Since my phone and I did witness you living on the wild side," I tease, patting my back pocket.

"But I trust you with my secrets. Especially the ones that could bite me in the ass."

Too hard to resist. I peer around at him, like I'm checking out his rear. "You do have a cute ass, Sullivan."

He growls lightly, and the sound sends tingles along my skin, especially when he murmurs, "So do you."

Soon, the steps turn into wooden stairs, then we reach a street sign for Napier Lane, a quiet block.

And it's . . . gorgeous, bursting with gardens and flowers and plants. "This is like a hamlet in the city," I say as we wander past several little cottages then along more gardens.

A bird squawks in a nearby tree. I point to the green-and-orange-winged creature. "I love the parrots of Telegraph Hill," I say.

He smiles at me, sunlight casting a dreamy afternoon glow across his handsome face. "Funny, I've heard about them, but never learned the story."

I square my shoulders, pride suffusing me. "I can tell you. Want to know?"

"Tell me a story, Erin," he says in that sultry tone that sends sparks down my chest.

"The parrot flock started in 1990 when a pair of small cherry-headed conures escaped and flew here."

"Where'd they escape from?"

I shrug. "Who knows? That's what I love about the story. No one truly knows, but everyone has a theory where the parrots came from."

I toss out some of my ideas:

Alcatraz.

Pier 39.

The Apple headquarters.

Sullivan jumps in, suggesting the Sutro Baths, Google, and Danielle Steel's house.

We wander down the block, trading tales about the wild parrots in the middle of a city.

"It's a parrot jungle in the metropolis," he remarks. "A conundrum—completely what you don't expect."

That tugs on the restless part of my mind, the part that craves deeper stories. "See? That's what I'd love to report on too. Finding the unexpected tale. The quirky little detail in a story that makes you sit up and take notice."

"Like when a baseball play doesn't go the way you think. When the shortstop appears out of nowhere and is suddenly fielding a ball on the first baseline," he muses.

"Or when a pitcher is good enough to be the designated hitter too, and he belts in the game-winning home run. Why is he so good at the plate too? Turns out he had to learn to hit, and if he hadn't, he never would have been able to play in his home country," I say.

We trade on and off like that, and then we do it again a few weeks later when we check out the Crissy Field stairs leading to the Golden Gate Bridge. On our next outing, we visit the Instagrammable tiled steps on Sixteenth Avenue that take us to a food truck where we devour tacos and talk more and more.

Like that, we discover the city, and we become better friends each weekend and on weeknights too—texting and talking.

Soon, fall turns into winter, and in January, our friend dates become more like lunches and dinners.

One night in early February, we head to an Italian restaurant in North Beach, and when he pulls out my chair, it feels more like a date-date.

And that feels risky. But the more time I spend with him, the more I'm embracing the risk.

The more I'm wanting something beyond friendship.

7

SULLIVAN

If I was grading myself, I'd give me an A.

Maybe that makes me cocky.

But I'm pretty sure it's accurate.

I've been an excellent student in the subject of Erin Madison.

And I've enjoyed every second of our friend dates. The stairs, the slides, the meals, the walks.

The wanderings.

Tonight at dinner is as good a time as any to let her in on a secret.

After we order and the waiter pours the wine, I offer my glass in a toast. "To friendship," I say, though that's not the secret.

"To friendship," she echoes, her voice warm, her eyes sparkling with happiness.

Exactly how I feel when I'm with her.

I take a drink of the wine, and she does the same, then licks her lips.

I narrow my eyes, humming my approval. "Mmm.

You look good doing that."

She dips her head, blushing. "So do you when you do that," she says when she looks at me again.

My chest heats from the compliment. "Glad you think so."

"But then, I find you attractive all the time," she says.

And yup, I'm hot everywhere now. "Can I tell you a secret?"

"Give it up, Sullivan," she says with a naughty twinkle in her eyes. I fucking love how she goes from sweet to dirty in a heartbeat.

"I love to read romance novels," I say, squaring my shoulders, owning it.

She laughs lightly, setting a hand on my forearm. A shiver rushes over my skin. Damn, I like it so much when she touches me.

"No one knows?" she asks.

"I keep it to myself. But I thought you'd enjoy knowing it."

"I do like that. I like all the details of you," she says.

And I am a certified goner for Erin Madison.

"Maybe someday you can do a story on Captain Romance," I say, then scoff at myself. "I call myself that. In my head."

She leans back in her chair, stifling a smile. "That's too cute."

Growling, I pretend to be mad. "Don't make me regret telling you."

"Hey! I *like* cute," she says, her eyes holding mine.

"So do I," I say, and it feels like we're talking about each other, about these feelings blooming between us, this friendship that's teetering on the verge of romance.

I hope.

I hope so damn much.

"Tell me your favorite romances," she says, and I do, sharing the details of some of the stories I've devoured.

"I detect a theme," Erin says, tapping her chin.

"And what's that?"

"They all have forbidden love, but they end in a happily ever after."

That's the great thing about stories—you can write the endings however you want.

But this is real life. I can imagine a romance with her —and maybe I am—but that doesn't bring me any closer to it happening.

When dinner ends, we walk through North Beach again, and I imagine doing this in a month, a few more months, a year.

Yes, I want to be friends with her.

I definitely want her in my life.

But I'm falling for her.

She's in my head, in my life, and in my heart.

Like we did that night in October, we meander, talking about the coming season. We talk about my friend Shane's trade from the New York Comets to the San Francisco Dragons, where he'll be playing with my buddy Drew, their catcher. Then we talk more about her job, and how she still wants to tell bigger stories. But we move on from work, chatting about music and friends as Stella's Comedy Attic comes into view.

She stops in front of it, checking out the marquee

and the list of upcoming acts. "Matilda Barker is going to be here this month," she says, pointing to the list of comics. "She's fabulous, and all my girlfriends love her. Clementine, Frankie, Nova . . ."

"You should go with them," I say, with some flirt in my tone.

"You should go too," she says, equally playful.

"Should we pretend to be surprised if we see each other?"

"We both love surprises," she says. Then she tilts her head, considering. "So, we'll act surprised."

"Great. If I run into you, I'll be shocked."

"It's a plan."

We turn away from the club, and I walk her home. My gaze keeps drifting to her hand, and the desire to hold it deepens, tunnels into my chest.

Drives me on.

"Can I hold your hand?" I ask, hopeful, but determined too.

She steals a glance at me, almost as if this moment is forbidden. "I was hoping you would."

I reach out, thread my fingers through hers, and murmur, "Nice."

"Very, very nice," she says, shooting me a sexy look.

Holding hands has never felt this right, or this intimate.

When we reach her home, I'm full of hope, wanting this night to be different, this chance to be the one.

It's time to tell her more. To lay my heart on the line.

On the front steps of her building, I imagine I'm heading out to the mound.

Determined, focused, ready.

The outcome of the game rests on my shoulders, and so does my future with Erin.

I draw a deep breath and then jump. "Erin, I don't want to put you in an uncomfortable situation, but I just want to tell you that I love being friends with you, and I also would love to take you out. On a regular basis. Not like a one-time thing." I go on, buoyed by the sparks in her blue eyes. "I want to be your man. Your boyfriend, if you'll have me. I'm not asking for a one-night stand, or a one-and-done date. I'm asking for you. And I know all the risk falls on you, but I'll be here for you to navigate those pitfalls. I'll be by your side however you need me, if you'll take that chance."

Her shoulders shudder slightly, maybe with happiness. Her hand flies to her mouth, then she lets go. "Oh God," she gasps in wonder. "Really?"

"Yes. Does that surprise you?" I ask with a laugh.

"It just makes me happy."

This seems like a chance worth taking. "You make me happy, Erin. And this whole wander-through-the-city thing feels like it could be you and me. Think about it. Think about us, okay?" I ask, and I just hope.

I hope so damn hard.

"I think about you all the time, Sullivan," she confesses.

Then, she's wildly fast. She rises up on tiptoe, and I expect a chaste kiss like I've given her many times before. But instead, she goes straight for my mouth—dives right in and kisses me.

It's soft at first, an exploration, her soft lips gliding

across mine. I let her lead because that's what she seems to want and because I'm not entirely sure where we're going. But this woman knows her mind. And evidently her body too. She inches closer, a mere heartbeat away, then she sets her hands on my face.

Ah, hell.

I reach for her hips, jerk her against me, and explore her mouth. My tongue skates against hers, our sighs mingling, and the one-time impossibility of us falls away as we kiss against the night. In the span of these delicious seconds, I'm imagining new scenarios for us, possibilities where this could be real.

When she breaks the kiss, I wait for her to take the lead again.

"I had to know," she says, a teasing light in her eyes.

"Had to know what?"

"If kissing you was as worth it as I'd hoped it would be."

I laugh. "And? Conclusion?"

"It feels like the start of a new story," she says. "I kind of want to spend all night with you. But I think I know what would happen if I did."

"What would happen?"

"I'd do all the naughty things I can't do quite yet."

"When, then?" I ask. I'm desperate, but thrilled, waiting on the edge of the world for her.

"I promise I'll tell you soon."

* * *

"Soon" comes by way of a text a week later, shortly before Valentine's Day.

Erin: I'm going to Stella's with my friends. I'll act surprised.

Sullivan: I'll do the same.

It feels like the end of our friend dates and the beginning of a real one.

8

SULLIVAN

My buddy Shane texts me that he'll be arriving in the city the next day. Since he's now a Dragon, he'll be moving here before we all take off for spring training.

Sullivan: Want a welcome parade? I'll see if I can round up your biggest fans. Wait, that's no one.

Shane: Guess I'll settle for a pint, then, with my mates. NOT YOU.

Drew jumps into the text fray.

Drew: I'll pretend to be your bud, Shakespeare, if you pay for the drinks.

Shane: What a wildly generous offer.

After that, we get around to planning a welcome-back-to-town night that just happens to fall on

February 14th. I mention the comedy club, but the day before the event, I suggest a concert too, knowing Shane will say no, since he's staying away from the club scene.

It's all a ruse.

On Valentine's Day, the three of us head to Stella's, catching up on the new Marvel flick releasing next week, and discussing whether we want to see it or not during spring training, which leads to a debate on the best superheroes, since we live for arguments.

It's good to see the guys, but my mind keeps jumping ahead as we walk to the club.

To Erin.

To tonight.

To what might happen, and whether we'll indulge in another kiss or maybe more.

Please let it be more.

Once we're seated in Stella's and the headliner takes the stage, my gaze catches on a table not far away.

There she is—the woman I spent so many days and nights with during the off-season.

Time spent getting to know her.

Getting to like her.

Falling for her.

As friends.

And now, I'm determined to be so much more than that.

We could be everything.

I just want to be worth the risk for her.

* * *

Matilda Barker strolls across the stage, mic in hand. "This last date I went on was great. When I said sit, they sat. When I said come . . ." She stops, smiling coyly. "Oh, please. It happens that way in romance novels. When the man goes all alpha commanding in bed and says, 'Come for me.'" Matilda rolls her eyes. "And the woman's like, 'Oh yes, yes, yes.' As if that works."

Erin chuckles from across the room. So does a tall redhead sitting beside her.

Shane snorts next to me.

Or maybe it's a laugh-snort.

I shoot him a look.

He just shrugs, then we return our focus to the stage as Matilda scans the audience, giving us an innocent look. "Anyway, he came when I said come . . . What? I wasn't gonna miss a chance with the brown-and-tan min pin." Matilda slides into the next bit. "The breakup took me a little longer. The person I was dating said, *I think you're just dating me for my dog.*" She stops, shrugging. "I mean . . . that's not wrong."

Shane snorts again, which makes me laugh harder, then I peer across the room, curious if Erin's still laughing too. She is.

That makes me smile.

When the set ends, I take out my phone to text her, but there's a note from her already blinking at me.

Erin: I need *and* want to talk to my friends for a bit, but I'm dying to see you. I have something to tell you soon. Don't leave.

Sullivan: Can't wait to hear, and I'll be here.

I spend the next hour debating Drew on the merits of Elmore Leonard versus Raymond Chandler.

After Shane and Clementine, one of Erin's friends, take off, Erin shoots me a secret smile, then mouths, *Hi.*

The timing seems right. I tip my chin toward Drew. "Need to go talk to someone," I tell him.

"Would that be Erin Madison?" he asks, ever so innocently.

I shoot him a stare. "Yes, why?"

He shrugs like he's got a big, juicy secret. "Nothing. Except for the fact that you were staring at her throughout the whole set."

I rein in a grin, my lips twitching. "I don't think so."

"I don't know why you're denying it. Dude, I get that you like her. And she's great. Just talk to her."

"I wasn't really looking for permission." I've been giving it to myself for some time now.

He arches a dubious brow. "Oh, you weren't? My mistake. I'll just ignore how you've been sitting here for hours, distracted as fuck, trying to figure out how to make your move after all this time."

My friend looks serene and smug, confident in his ability to read the situation. He's not far off, but I won't give him the satisfaction of knowing that yet.

"Well, on that note," I say, "I'm heading over."

Once I'm walking to her table, though, sudden nerves cause a knot in my chest. Nothing has officially changed since the last time I saw her, but it feels like everything is about to.

I reach the table, and all the ladies look up at me. "Hey, Erin," I say.

A redhead smirks.

A woman with heart-shaped glasses smiles coyly.

Erin flashes a wildly delighted grin as she runs her hand through her hair. "Hey, Sullivan."

"Did you enjoy the show?"

"I did."

"And it sure seems like my friend Shane enjoyed chatting with Clementine," I say, gesturing to the door.

The redhead chimes in with a pointed question. "Is that why you're coming to talk to Erin?"

Erin gestures to her auburn-haired friend. "This is Nova. She's in charge of pretty much everything," Erin says as she rolls her eyes.

Nova waves hello at me. The woman in the glasses introduces herself as Frankie, and I swear her eyes drift over to the table where I was, almost like she's connecting with Drew.

But maybe the romance novels I listen to are putting those ideas into my head.

Either way, I need to rely on instinct for my romance right the fuck now. Captain Romance is here. "Erin, can I steal you away?"

"I was hoping you would," she says, then tells her friends goodbye.

"Get it, girl," Nova says.

"If you talk to Clementine, tell her I'll catch her up on everything," Erin says.

As we leave, I arch a brow. "Everything? I'm intrigued."

"Good. It involves you," she says, wrapping her hand around my arm.

I practically race out of the club. "Serve it up. I want to know everything, *friend*," I say as we hit the sidewalk.

"Walk with me," she says, and I'll follow her anywhere. "Want to know what I did during the off-season?"

"Hung out with me?"

"Besides that."

I'm champing at the bit. "Yes, I really do."

"I explored the city," she says, almost like she's a little bit shy or maybe nervous to tell me that. Like she's opening herself up to me. Sharing something private—even though I was with her on some of those explorations.

"Beyond where we went together?"

She nods. "Every day, I visited off-the-beaten-path spots. Hidden gems. Researched the places I didn't know. Learned the history. And then I made my pitch."

I'm buzzed, and I haven't had a single drop of alcohol. This story is going somewhere. Somewhere good.

Somewhere incredible.

I feel it in my bones. In my gut. "What's the pitch? I do love pitches."

She stops in her tracks, and I stop too. Reaching for my shirt collar, Erin tugs me close. "I'm no longer the beat reporter for the Cougars. I'm now hosting and producing documentaries for my network."

My jaw drops.

Surprising me is hard. But she just did it. "You are?" It comes out staccato with shock.

"I am. I start in two weeks. I was making mini documentaries on my own about sports and the city and local icons. The network loved them, and they're making a new job for me." She wraps her arms around my neck, playing with the ends of my hair. "They told me yesterday, and I wanted to tell you tonight. You're not a conflict of interest anymore, because I won't be covering your team every day. I can be with you, if you'll have me."

I'm so jazzed up, I can barely stand still. I can barely think. I can only feel. And I feel great. "Will you be mine?"

She just smiles, soft and shy. "Yes. I'm yours. Will you take me home tonight?"

We're gone in a heartbeat.

9

ERIN

I'm not making this change for him.

It's for me.

I'm doing this because I learned something that night we spent together at the end of last season. I learned what I truly want in my career. I learned, too, that you have to go after what you want. What makes you happy in life, love, and work.

But I'm the kind of person who needs evidence and proof.

I needed to know what my own restlessness was all about.

I started to discover the answer when Sullivan told me stories about his family, then showed me parts of the city I didn't know. I began to connect the dots, to figure out what I'd been yearning for.

As we explored more, I assembled the clues, determined I was ready for a chance. I knew I wanted to shift away from the day-in-and-day-out grind, and to tell the human-interest tales.

I proved myself, producing and reporting on my own, developing a portfolio, then showing it to my boss.

I loved every second of the work, and she did too.

But the best part is this—getting the guy.

Having it all.

Tonight, though, I'd like something in particular.

Sex, for the first time.

When we reach my home, I tug him into my place, shut the door, then set my hands on his shoulders.

I'm not embarrassed.

I'm not ashamed.

But I want him to know who I am.

"I'm a virgin, and I really want you to be my first, Sullivan Fitzgerald."

His eyes go hazy and wildly sexy. "I want that so much."

10

SULLIVAN

But there's more to say than *yes*. When I take Erin to the bedroom and strip off her shirt, reveling in her tight, toned athletic frame, I set the record straight.

"I want you so much, and I need you to know I will be making love to you," I tell the woman I'm mad about. "You want to know why?"

She trembles, a shudder running through her body. "Why?"

I cup her cheek, thrilling in the privilege of touching her like this at last. "Because I'm in love with you, Erin Madison. I fell in love with you when we were friends. When we roamed the city. When we did everything."

Her eyes shine. "And I fell in love with you."

And now we fall into bed, clothes flying all the way off as we go.

We kiss madly, and it's like a whole new type of kissing. It's deep and long and needy. It feels like it won't end, like it's a brand-new beginning as we come together like this.

We've been hoping for this. Craving each other.

I don't want it to end, so I don't stop kissing as my hands roam down her body, traveling over her breasts. They journey along the soft flesh of her stomach then between her legs, where I happily, so damn happily, slide my fingers through her silky wetness.

I groan as I touch her.

Her hands grab at my pecs when I trace her heat.

And we are off to the races as I touch her like I cherish her.

She writhes as my hands explore her, her reactions making my cock harder, my need wilder.

She responds like a dream, moaning into my kisses, then breaking apart, calling my name as she bucks and thrusts into my hand.

Soon she's coming on my fingers, shuddering beautifully.

I savor all of her pleasure, and a minute later, she's gazing at me, her eyes lust-drunk as she thrusts a condom my way and then gives me an order. "On your back."

I do love a woman who knows her mind and body. "Yes, ma'am."

I oblige, flopping onto my back, running a fist down my cock, then covering myself with protection.

Straddling me, she looks like a determined goddess. She rubs the head of my dick against her, tossing her head back, her neck stretching. She moans a sexy *oh God*.

Then she stares hotly at me.

"I've thought about you fucking me a lot, Sullivan. Thought about your cock filling me," she rasps.

Holy fuck. My Erin is a sexy vixen, and I love it. "What a filthy, beautiful mouth you have."

"I have a dirty mind, and I'm not afraid to use it."

"Use me. Use my dick all you want," I urge her, holding the base, offering my shaft for her to ride.

"I will," she says, then she goes slowly, lowers herself, and takes just the tip.

She tenses. Her expression shifts to one of pain.

"You okay, baby?" I ask.

She nods, her lips tight. "I'll be okay."

"Take it slow," I tell her gently.

"I will," she says, and she draws a deep breath, then exhales, sinking deeper.

Her jaw ticks. She draws another breath, then she's all the way on me.

And she feels incredible. "You feel so fucking good, baby."

"So do you," she says on a shudder.

I grip her hips, holding her as she sets the pace, slow and easy at first—nice and tender. I lift my face, kissing her lush lips as she finds a rhythm.

As we move together, we kiss like we're making up for all that time. Making it up in kisses and sex, in sex and kisses.

We're tangled together, moaning and thrusting, fucking and loving.

And the woman I proved myself to is coming on top of me.

It's glorious and loud and so damn good.
I follow her there, blissed out and in love.
This is the way to start a new season.
With a friend and a lover, all in one.

EPILOGUE

Erin

The next morning, with spring training beginning, I stay behind in the city, and that feels just right.

So does going to see my friends at Doctor Insomnia, where I catch them up on my new job over coffee.

"You are a badass babe," Nova declares.

Clementine gives me a fist bump.

Frankie hoots. "Sometimes you just have to go after what you want," she says. "Trust me on this."

"Oh, I do trust you. Because you're all about that," I say, since Frankie shared some secrets with me over text today.

Nova pats my knee. "You seem happy. Less . . . restless."

I beam. "Yes! Exactly. This is what I really want. And the time I spent with Sullivan helped me to see that."

"I'm so stinking happy for you," Frankie says, and all my friends echo her sentiment.

"I'm happy too," I say, feeling so much more than content.

Feeling just right about everything.

* * *

When Sullivan returns from spring training, I don't go to his season opener as a reporter.

I go in the capacity of my brand-new job, making documentaries on sports, and people, and this city.

Not him.

Not the Cougars.

And it's wonderful to have it all.

He wins the first game, and afterward we wander through the city.

But not for too long.

Because I learned something else I love doing after midnight.

Getting naked with the man I love.

THE END

KISS YOUR TULIPS

A FRANKIE AND DREW SHORT STORY

1

DREW

If I weren't a ball player, I could be a doctor.

Why?

I'm not squeamish.

I've got a good bedside manner—well, I have good manners in bed, and that has to count.

And my handwriting is atrocious.

I mean, consider the to-do list I wrote myself last night.

I take it from the magnet on the fridge and pour my morning joe, trying to read my writing.

Gut pony . . .

What on earth is a gut pony?

I shudder at the thought of the poor equine and his tummy trouble as I take a thirsty gulp of my brew. I need the coffee to sharpen my brain as I try to decipher the next item on my to-do list. Does that say . . .

Muddy tools?

Did I plan a home improvement project before I conked out last night? Sure, I like to putter around my home and build birdhouses, but I don't need dirty tools for that.

But why would I write *this*?

Piss ice.

I didn't even drink last night.

Fine, I had one glass of wine with my best friend, Jenna.

Still, this shit is weird, even for me.

Yet clearly, this was important enough to write down. Admittedly, it was a late night. Jenna was bummed, so I took her out for dinner, wine, and all the cake, just like she did for me a couple years ago when Holly dumped me.

It's a thing—we've helped each other through breakups and makeups and everything else since we were kids. Her douche-nozzle of a dickweed ex-husband cheated on her, and now she's facing the hellscape of online dating.

Maybe this note was about her?

Think like a detective, Drew.

I study my handwriting again.

"Ah, yes! You are Sam Spade," I say.

Get peonies, maybe tulips, possibly irises.

Yup. Call me Robert Langdon. I'm a motherfucking code breaker—and the world's best childhood bud. Jenna loves flowers, so it's time to cheer her up with some petals.

Valentine's Day is in seven days, and I'm going to take her mind off her snake of an ex.

After I shower and get dressed, I Google "flower

delivery," but then kill that idea. I've no idea what kind to get her.

I know nothing about flowers.

But there's a cute flower shop next to the hardware store I frequent. Can't remember its name, but I can ask the florist there for advice.

On my way from my place in Pacific Heights, I swing past Doctor Insomnia's Tea And Coffee Emporium, where I spot some familiar faces—my teammates from the Dragons Declan and Holden, along with Declan's husband, Grant, who catches for the Cougars.

I pop in to say hello to the trio and they draw me into their discussion of the upcoming season. "This year, we're going to win it all," I say to Declan and Holden.

"We damn well better," Declan says.

"We're going all the way," Holden agrees.

"I can feel it in my bones." Sure, I'm Mister Optimistic—it's the only way to be when you play a game for a living.

Grant shakes his head. "Don't be so cocky. I'd bet on the Cougars."

"Of course you would." I scoff at the rival backstop. After some good-natured smack-talk, I take off, telling Declan and Holden I'll see them in a week.

Spring is the best time of year—the earth seems to wake from its long winter's nap, pitchers and catchers report for training, and baseball begins anew.

It's a world full of promise.

A season for new starts.

I've been catching for the Dragons for four seasons now, and every year, I'm sure we're going to win it all.

I head down Fillmore, and soon I spot the shop I'm after. The place is teeming with buds, the curbside display bursting with buckets of flowers, full of pink and orange and fiery petals. They are gorgeous and I know zip about them.

But hey, that's what florists are for.

I read the cute wooden sign hanging on a chain under a green awning.

Kiss Your Tulips.

Sounds like my kind of flower shop. I love a good pun. I walk inside, inhaling the scent of—I'm guessing here—roses, lilies, and carnations. Then my eyes land on a vivacious spark of a woman amid the blooms.

And I take my sweet time cataloging *her.*

The woman behind the counter.

The first thing I notice is her smile.

It's inviting. Kind. A little clever, too, as she interacts with the customers.

Then there's her glasses, candy-apple red, and heart-shaped, and her hair, long and silky, falling in black waves along her shoulders.

A pink apron cinched at her waist says *I lilac you* in embroidery across the bib.

Yup. Already, I lilac her style.

She arranges some brilliant orange and sun-yellow flowers in a mint-green vase, chatting with an older lady. "If you want to set your mouth on fire, get the Super Spicy Eggplant Tofu. Your lips will go up in flames." She shares a conspiratorial smile along with the recommendation. "What more could you ask for on Valentine's Day than fire and spice?"

What do you know? I love spicy eggplant tofu. Spicy eggplant steak. Spicy veggies drizzled in hot sauce. Spice is the spice of life.

The customer thanks her for the tip and then heads to the door, a bell tinkling as she exits.

I step up to the green wooden counter, read the spice lover's name tag, and flash a grin.

I'm Mister Optimistic, after all, and I'm hoping she's as clever as she is cute.

"Hey, there, Frankie. I'm Drew, and I'm clueless about flowers."

She meets my gaze, her smile both flirty and a bit devilish. "Then it's a good thing you met me."

It sure feels that way.

2

FRANKIE

When people learn I own a flower shop, they almost always make the same observation, sometimes phrased as a question.

You must really love flowers, right?

Well, yeah. Would I open a cupcake shop if I didn't love treats?

(Newsflash—I adore treats. I'm not a monster.)

I love lots of things—frosting, sunrise, good friends, the smell of fresh-brewed coffee, food so spicy it burns, wordplay, and raucous laughter. I love fishnet stockings like the burgundy pair I'm wearing right now, kick-ass lace-up boots, plus sex, orgasms, and men with humor and brains who can deliver the latter.

Also, I love flowers.

Flowers are a medium for people to connect.

They're a way to say *I'm thinking of you,* to cheer up someone who's sad, to show sympathy for someone's loss.

They're an explosion of color to celebrate a friend's accomplishment.

I love, too, when people buy flowers for themselves, just because they're pretty, just because they want to be surrounded by beauty.

Flowers are one of the best *just becauses* out there.

Most of all, I love when flowers are an expression of love.

That's why Valentine's Day is one of my favorite times of the year. The seven days before it I call "Eye Candy Week," when hot guy after hotter guy wanders into my store on a tell-someone-I-love-them mission.

Guys like Drew, with those sea-blue eyes, that thick, dark hair, those full lips, and that jawline that belongs on a magazine cover. I swear, there is something in the water in this neighborhood, and it's growing beautiful men.

I sure hope the water company keeps using it, since I do love the view.

But first, business.

"So, Drew, tell me all about your botanical needs, and I can help you *once and floral*," I say.

He chuckles. "You give good pun."

I cup the side of my mouth. "Insider secret—I memorized all the good flower puns when I opened the shop."

"An excellent use of your time, since I imagine you *rose to the occasion*."

Be still, my flirty, dirty beating heart.

He's all silver-tongued and sexy.

"Of course I did," I say, trying like hell to contain a grin, but finding that impossible. I kinda can't resist a word-flinger. But, resist I must. "Now, what are you looking for?"

"A bouquet a day for the next week," he says.

Holy romance. Drew has it going on.

"But can you help me pick them out? I am batting zero when it comes to flowers."

"No worries," I say. "I'll make your *daisy* with my selection."

He slow-claps. "Damn, Frankie. You are the goddess of flower puns."

"Speaking of goddesses . . . the iris is fitting." I gesture to a framed photo of a gorgeous garden full of irises on the wall behind me. "She's the goddess of rainbows, so those flowers can be quite regal, though not entirely a Valentine's bloom. Personally, I love tulips in all shades, but you can't go wrong this time of year with gerbera daisies, lilies, carnations, or"—I motion to our cold case of roses bursting with red, pink, and white petals—"the classic rose."

Tapping his chin, he studies the selection. "I want something other than roses. Something that says I did my research with the florist," he says, giving me a wink.

And that wink sends a tingle down my chest.

Oh, how very wrong of me to feel all tingly for a customer who's likely buying flowers for another woman.

I wheel around to the next case, but before I can show him the lilies, his attention catches on a wire rack of greeting cards illustrated with fruit, veggies, and flowers. Laughing, he points to a drawing of an eggplant, reading the caption. *"Are you checking out my junk?"* His eyes meet mine. "Is that a popular card you send with flowers?"

I pick up the ivory card with the purple veggie. "It's actually one of my top sellers. Never underestimate the value of a naughty note to go with a beautiful bouquet," I tell him.

"Big fan of naughty notes," he says with a rasp to his voice, like he's downshifted to a sexy tone.

Come to think of it, he's kind of sounded like sex the whole time he's been here—another reason why my skin is a little toasty near this hottie. "Then you should hear what I *almost* put on that card," I whisper.

He shoots me a dirty grin. "Serve it up, Frankie."

Should I go for it? Ah, what the hell. I hold up the card that caught his attention and quote myself. "'The eggplant often wondered if it should return to its original name—*the dick fruit.*'"

Drew bursts into laughter. Peals of it. "Dick fruit. Damn, woman. You have a beautifully dirty mind."

I tap the side of my temple. "And I don't waste it." I show him another eggplant card that says, *"Nice junk."*

"I approve of this selection of cards," he says, picking up a banana one. *"The first rule of eating a banana—don't make eye contact."* The man with the sea-blue eyes shoots me the naughtiest stare. "But I'm all for eye contact, Frankie."

And the sizzle turns into a flame. His gaze lights me

up. Yup, I like spicy things, like the fire in his blue eyes. Like the way he stares at me.

Like the . . .

Snap out of it, Frankie!

He's a customer.

I fix on a professional grin, erasing the last few minutes, and change the mood. "So, what flowers would you like for the first day?"

He sighs a little wistfully. "I'm not sure. See, there's this girl. We've been best friends forever, and the flowers are for her."

Knew it. He was too good to be true. Though, why would he give me sex eyes when he's sending flowers to someone else? Ugh. Men are more confusing than math sometimes.

He hands the banana card to me. "Maybe we should start with the message first."

"Sure. Would you like a pen to write a note to your *friend*?"

Oops. That might have come out sarcastically.

Who cares if he made an eye-contact comment sound seductive? He's not doing anything wrong. *Just settle down and be the cupid you are. Don't cock block him.*

Drew gives me pleading eyes. "I was hoping you could write the note. I have the world's worst handwriting."

I arch a brow. "The worst? I've seen some pretty bad handwriting, mister."

"Oh, trust me." He fishes a crinkled Post-it note from his jeans pocket, unfolds the yellow paper, and shows it to me.

I study it, untangling the letters like solving a word jumble.

"Get peonies. Maybe tulips. Possibly irises." I pause like that's my *Jeopardy!* answer and I'm waiting for the official ruling.

His eyes widen. His jaw comes unhinged. Then he mimes an explosion. "You are a rock star at handwriting deciphering," he says.

I laugh. "It's one of my many skills. I'm also really good at puzzles, logic problems, and crosswords, so I consider handwriting interpretation in the same family of sleuthing."

"Moment of truth—did you love Nancy Drew or The Hardy Boys when you were growing up?"

"Please. That's child's play. I teethed on them. By the time I was ten, I was Hercule Poirot all the way. Agatha Christie is my jam."

Drew clutches his chest like he's thrilled. "I'm a Dashiell Hammett man, myself," he says. "Sam Spade is my guy."

A reader. How delicious. He's going to make this woman so very happy. "Women really do like a man who enjoys books," I say.

"I'm excellent at compliments too," he says, and nods to the card. "This is what I want to say to her: *You are brilliant and amazing.* Can you add *Love, Drew*?"

I'm already swooning on her behalf as I return to the counter to ring up his purchase and write his card. "I can definitely do that. And what kind of flowers do you want?"

"What kind would *you* like to get?"

"Oh," I say, stopping behind the counter. "Hardly anyone asks me that. They mostly just want me to be a flower matchmaker—or maybe a psychic—and tell them what the other person would want."

He shoots me a warm grin. "Then tell me what flowers you like. Jenna likes everything."

Lucky Jenna. She gets flowers and a witty guy with eyes that melt me. I mean, *her*. I bet those eyes melt her.

And her panties.

"Gerbera daisies are a good bet," I say.

"Daisies it is."

"And for the rest of the week? Do you want to place your orders for those now?"

"Good question. The alternative is coming in each day to pick?"

"Yes. We get deliveries each day, so you might spot something you love. But I'm happy to take all the orders now."

He waits a beat, strokes his chin. "I'm a let-the-mood-strike-me kind of guy, so let's do it every morning," he says, and I try not to think of doing *him* each morning.

Even though . . . *morning sex*. Yum.

"Sounds like a plan." I write on the card and show it to him.

"Your handwriting is as good as your instinct to forgo the dick-fruit joke," he says, with a wink.

A wink that I wish was truly for me.

"Someday, the dick fruit will have its moment in the sun," I say solemnly.

"But if a dick were out in the sun, is that indecent exposure?"

I laugh. "The very definition of it."

"I thought it might be. See you tomorrow, Frankie," he says.

Already, I wish it were tomorrow. Looks like Eye Candy Week is living up to its reputation.

3

DREW

For the record, I don't believe in love at first sight when it comes to anything except baseball.

Okay, fine. Maybe books. I have definitely fallen in love with books from the first page.

And movies from the opening shot.

Also, shit. Songs from the beginning notes.

But women? I don't fall quickly for a woman. I like to take my time getting to know her, to understand her.

And by her, I mean Frankie, the naughty florist.

I stroll inside Kiss Your Tulips the next morning, get in line, and wait my turn.

Frankie bustles behind the counter, arranging a bouquet of lilies, I think, as she chats with an elderly gentleman. "She's going to be so happy when she gets these, Mr. Caruso," she says.

"Mrs. Caruso makes me happy every day," he says.

"And that's why you bring home her favorite stargazers. It's simpatico," she says.

"It absolutely is," he says.

Frankie's grin lights up the store—no, the whole damn block—as she smiles then pushes her glasses up higher on her nose.

The glasses are so very her. Quirky, flirty, and fun.

Dammit. I'm getting ahead of myself. I know nothing about Frankie. Maybe she's married, or she doesn't like dick fruit.

As she finishes with Mr. Caruso, I flick through the cards.

"Someday, you'll find your very own person who makes you happy every day," he says.

Oh, Fate. Hello.

I listen intently.

"Someday, indeed. I haven't met him yet, but I bet he's out there," she says, and I want to kiss the sky.

Single, and she's a fan of dick fruit. Yay me.

Pleased with my easy detective work, I pick a new card for Jenna—an illustration of a pineapple and the words, *"You are one fine apple."*

When it's my turn at the counter, I meet her brown-eyed gaze. "Good morning, Frankie. We have to stop meeting like this," I say, teasing.

"I do get the impression you're *stalking* this place," she says as she holds up the stalk of a sunflower.

"Damn. You can organize bouquets like nobody's business and come up with the puns like that." I snap my fingers.

"I told you it's one of my skills."

"And you won't ever get . . . *clover* it," I say.

Her eyes sparkle. "The student is becoming the expert."

"I'm a fast learner. Also, this card is gold." I set it on the counter. "Was your first draft something about how drinking pineapple juice every day makes all that eye contact taste better?"

"*Shhh.*" She places a finger on her lips. "Who's naughty now?"

I shrug. "It's my middle name. Drew Naughty McBride."

"How prescient of your parents."

"I like to think so," I say, then tap the card. "I trust this is your brainchild? Since it's a little bit naughty."

She gives a coquettish little bob of her shoulder. "All mine."

"So, you draw the cards too? You're a triple threat?"

"How does that add up? I count flower arranging and illustrating cards. What's the third threat?"

I scoff then point to the cup of pens on the counter. "Don't sell yourself short, Frankie. You've got hella good handwriting."

She flicks strands of silky black hair off her shoulder. "I should enter the Penmanship World Championship."

"You know what? You joke about that, but I bet there is a Penmanship World Championship."

She lifts a dubious brow. "Are you sure about that? That seems really specific."

"Want to bet on it?"

"What are we betting for?"

"Bragging rights," I say, like it's obvious.

"Okay, fine," she says, laughing, waving in my direction. "Do it. Google 'Penmanship World Championship.'"

I whip out my phone, tap that into Google, and show it to her. "See? There is one."

She peers from the screen to me, narrowing her eyes. "Huh. Not bad. But how do I know you didn't come in here prepped to set me up?"

"If I did, I should get a major gold star for planning ahead. Because *I* only mentioned handwriting. *You* wanted to be World Champion."

"Hmm. That *would* be some serious commitment, preparing a punchline for any scenario," she says. Then she takes a deep breath, flashes me a professional smile. "What do you want to send your friend today?"

Checking out the flower displays, I pocket my phone. "Can you pick again? Maybe your favorites? Or second favorites."

"I happen to love lilies," she says.

"Lilies it is," I agree, then hand her a pen from the cup. "And on this card can you write: *You couldn't be any more pear-fect?*"

Frankie shoots me an approving grin. "Who's the king of puns now?"

I hold up a hand in surrender. "Fine, fine. I might have Googled fruit puns too."

"I'm giving you points *and* gold stars for using Google to the fullest today."

I take a bow. "Thank you. Thank you very much." As she arranges the flowers, I tell her how much Jenna loved the first bouquet. "She'll love these too. I just really want to make her happy, you know?"

Frankie tilts her head and shoots me a soft smile. "That's really sweet—that you feel that way."

She writes the card and gets it ready to be couriered to Jenna's house.

That night, Jenna tells me how much better she's feeling already.

And my week goes on like that.

I go to the store every day. I ask Frankie to pick out her favorite flowers. I chat and flirt with her, getting to know her a little bit more.

A woman like that, who's clever and open, who loves the meaning behind flowers and loves plays on words, who likes to make bawdy jokes, and who always has a kind word for customers?

She's the kind of a woman who deserves a big gesture early on.

4

FRANKIE

I am the worst. That's what I tell my bestie, Nova, two nights before Valentine's Day as I flop onto a couch beside her at The Spotted Zebra. "I'm totally crushing on this customer who's sending notes to his"—I stop to sketch air quotes—"'best friend.'"

Nova's blue eyes spark with curiosity as she takes a swallow of her mojito. "All right, confessional time. Tell your high priestess. I want to know everything that's going on with this forbidden fruit."

I give her the lowdown on Drew, the blue-eyed babe. "He's witty and funny and a little bit dirty."

Nova gives an approving nod. "We dirty girls like the dirty ones," she says.

I high-five her. "I love a man who comes across like he has no weird sex rules, or dating rules, and that's totally the vibe I get from him."

She raises both hands. "Preach it. Well, I like a woman that way."

I laugh. "I know, and you reel 'em in."

"True, I do," she says, all confident, and with good reason.

"Plus, we have these great conversations, but he's clearly taken because he's sending flowers every day to the same woman."

"That is so berry sweet," she says, playing up the sap.

I shove her shoulder. "Why do you always make fun of me?"

"Because it's easy." She sets down her mojito, her expression going serious. "But I want details. Tell me more about the notes."

"They're very endearing. But so is he. And I'm falling into a crush that's surely going nowhere," I say, grabbing her drink and downing the rest of it.

She pulls a face. "Maybe so, but *you* are going to the bar to get me a new drink."

I head to the bar, grab two more mojitos, and we toast to single men and women who are dirty, flirty, and loyal.

* * *

The next morning, like clockwork, Drew's at the shop, looking sexy in jeans and a navy-blue Henley, his magazine-cover face knocking the breath out of me.

Yup, he's now on that list of things I like.

I'm going to need a new fantasy, stat, since I took him for a ride in my dirty dreams last night.

Drew rubs his palms together like a coach gearing up for the big game. "All right, this is the last one, Frankie. What should I send her?"

I take a deep breath, focusing on just the right flowers for his lucky friend. "Well, you said Jenna likes anything."

"Yes, but I really want to know what *you* would want," he says, pointing at me.

My stomach flutters. My chest flips. Why does he have to be taken? "I love all flowers, but I like tulips the best."

He rocks back and forth on his heels. "Why's that?"

Ah, the chance to wax on about something I love. This is easy. "Because you can use tulips to say *I'm falling for you*. You can use tulips to say *I love you*. You can use them to say *I want to get you naked right now*. You can use them to say *You make my heart flutter*."

His lips twitch in a knowing grin. His blue eyes twinkle with possibilities. I am in this crush so damn deep. "And what if you want to ask somebody out on a date?"

Ugh, it's like a gut punch. I knew all along that was what he'd been leading up to with Jenna, but it still hurts to hear it. "I would send pink ones then."

"Sold." He turns to flick through the cards and picks one with a simple picture of a cherry. Inside it, he asks me to write this down.

You're funny. You're fabulous. You're beautiful. Would you like to go out with me sometime?

With my heart both jumping and plummeting, I write that down, then meet his eyes. "She's going to say yes," I tell him, smiling and doing my best to mean it.

"And why do you say that?"

I'm sure my expression is full of this helpless longing

I feel for him. "It's a no-brainer. I would love to be romanced like this."

That smile of his grows wider and wider. "Good to know."

My chest twists. "Same address as the other ones? To Jenna?" An embarrassing lump forms in my throat. It's so ridiculous that I've formed this attachment to this man.

Drew shakes his head. "Nope. Let me get the address. Be right back."

What the . . .?

I blink as he heads for the street, the bell tinkling as he exits. He stands in front of the shop, peers up above the door, then . . .

Walks back in.

Straight to me.

He stops at the counter, and he rattles off this address.

I stop mid-letter, pen frozen in hand. "Here?" It comes out in a squeak of surprise.

"Yes, and please address them to Frankie."

A riot ignites in my heart. "Yes! I say yes!"

That night, I wait for her outside the restaurant, grinning when I spot her. She walks up looking sexy and quirky and cute in an off the shoulder top, a short skirt, biker boots, and black stockings that worship the sexiest legs I've ever had the pleasure of viewing.

I stare shamelessly, and her eyes tell me she's got plenty of dirty ideas in her head too.

"A peony for your thoughts?" she asks.

I loop a hand around her hip. "You're simply *iris-istible.*"

"Ditto. Also, you win the best ask-out ever."

That's reason enough to kiss her. Well, kiss her cheek. Manners and all. I brush my lips across her soft skin, whispering, "Good. Because a week ago, I met this woman I really wanted to impress. And I'm so glad you said yes to this Valentine's Eve date."

We head into the restaurant and indulge in spicy eggplant tofu.

The date is fantastic.

We dine and talk, laugh and tease. She asks me about Jenna, and I tell her how she's doing.

"The flowers definitely cheered her up after her big breakup. She's a great friend. We grew up together on the same block, and we've always had each other's back."

Frankie sighs like she's relieved. "Confession: I thought you were romancing her with the flowers."

The idea surprises a laugh out of me. "No. She's truly a friend. And I have a confession too: I wanted to romance you from the second I walked into your shop."

"Good. I like your brand of romance," she says, then she asks what I do for a living, and when I tell her I play pro ball, her jaw drops. "I had no idea. I know nothing about sports."

"Good. Very good."

"Why?"

"It means you said yes because you like my . . . *junk mail.*"

She eyes me suspiciously. "But I haven't seen your junk mail, Drew." Then she leans across the table. "I want to though. And I'm kind of into eye contact, so I was thinking maybe we could . . ."

I jump on that. No way am I letting this chance pass me by. "Go back to my place?"

She smiles widely, nodding. "And do you think you could give me a couple orgasms? I really like orgasms."

"What do you know? I really like giving them."

* * *

But first things first.

Like kisses.

After dinner, out on the street, I cup her face. As a small rush of air escapes her lips, I move closer and press a soft kiss to her mouth. But soft only works for so long. Soon, the kiss darts up to another level. It's hotter and hungrier as my hand loops into her hair, wrapping those lush strands around my fingers.

She kisses me back with fierce determination. I raise the stakes—more roughness, more heat. I back her up against the brick building, my hands traveling down her sides.

She moves with me, all hands and lips too. She yanks me closer, sealing her body against mine, letting me know she wants all the same things I do.

When she lets go, she whispers, "Like I said, tulips can mean *I want to get you naked right now.*"

This is even better than baseball.

Better than spring training.

Better than winning.

Thirty minutes later, we're in my home, naked and tangled in my sheets, and I am the luckiest fucker in all of San Francisco because Frankie is between my legs, sucking me off, and I am dying from pleasure. Just dying with lust as she stares at me while she takes me deep.

But I won't ruin the night by coming too soon.

So as much as it pains me, I stop her, bring her close, and tell her it's time for me to give her my version of a triple threat.

"Is that three orgasms?"

"It absolutely is."

I deliver the first with my tongue, the second with my fingers, and I intend to give her the third with my cock.

Just how I think she'll like it.

"On your hands and knees, Frankie," I tell her.

She practically purrs her answer, "You know my naughty side."

"Know it. Want to feed it. Fucking love it." I move behind her, cover myself, and slide into her sweet heat, savoring the tight, hot feel of her. And we fuck, and nothing about it is the one-night stand variety.

We indulge in sex that's hot and uninhibited. That's shameless and wild. That involves tongues and teeth and dirty words.

Sex that lasts all night long.

That leaves me exhausted.

But not so much I forget my manners.

I ask before I pull her hair, before I spank her, before I squeeze and knead her ass.

And Frankie's answers are the best ever.

She says *yes, oh God, yes, and please, yes*.

In the morning, on Valentine's Day, I tell her I'm going to a comedy club with some of my friends tonight and ask if she'd like to meet up.

"I'd love to see you and your dick fruit again."

"Baby, I'm gonna need more of your sweet peaches," I say, and we laugh.

Then I take her out for breakfast, walk her to her store, and wish her a happy Valentine's Day.

* * *

I steal glances at Frankie throughout the comic's set, including when Matilda slides into her bit about online dating and dog fishing. "The breakup took me a little longer. The person I was dating said *I think you're just dating me for my dog.*" She stops, shrugs. "I mean . . . that's not wrong."

My teammate Shane snort-laughs, and I mock him for it.

But this comic is gold, so I get it.

I'm laughing too.

And, huh, so is the owner of my team—Marlow Winters, who's here with . . . holy shit . . . Hudson Tanner, the dude who owns the Cougars.

There might be a story there, and I file it away to consider later. Right now, I focus on Frankie. She's laughing and having a good time with her friends, and at the end of the evening, she's smiling when I walk over and ask if she wants to spend the night with me.

"Only if you promise to spank me hard again."

Like I said, a naughty mind is a terrible thing to waste.

* * *

The next six weeks, we text and talk and FaceTime during spring training. I catch up with Jenna too. She tells me she met a nice guy and is happier. She demands to know everything about Frankie, so I tell her about the woman I'm falling for.

When I return to San Francisco, I invite the naughty florist to my first game.

After our win, I take Frankie out for spicy food and hot kisses. I've missed her so damn much. On the street, as the spring breeze blows past us, I pull her in close. "I'm falling in love with you."

"Good. Because I'm already there."

I take her home that night, glad I figured out that my *two lips* were the key to her heart.

THE END

LIMO BANG

A BILLIONAIRE BETS SHORT STORY

1

MARLOW

A year ago

The night of the Sports Network Awards

When I bought the beleaguered, scandal-ridden San Francisco Dragons, I expected the biggest challenge of my career.

I had to turn around a team that had become the scourge of pro sports.

They'd won two tainted World Series' all because they were cheaters.

I hate cheaters.

Like, oh, say, my ex-husband.

But he's history, and I came out ahead in the divorce thanks to my shark of an attorney, who made sure I had the one thing all lady billionaires need before they get hitched—an iron-clad prenup.

My ex didn't get a single red cent.

My reward for kicking him to the curb a few years ago?

This team.

I'd always wanted to own a baseball team, ever since I was a little girl and my parents took me to see the New York Comets.

I rooted for the men in pinstripes, learned how to keep score at a game, and studied the farm system for the organization.

Once I made my first ten billion, thanks to launching one of the world's biggest online retailers, I set my sights on acquiring a baseball team.

The Dragons came up for sale, and now, they're mine.

My prize.

My passion.

My reward.

And I'm doing my damnedest to turn this team around, to rebuild its reputation and make it the glory of baseball again.

Which means the last thing I need is the distraction of a man.

Trouble is . . . *that guy over there.*

The one across the glittery ballroom at this awards gala, owner of the other baseball team in San Francisco.

My rival.

Hudson Tanner is decked out in his tux, all suave and sexy. His dark eyes pin me from his spot in the corner.

He stares at me like he doesn't just want to undress me, but like he already knows what I look like naked.

My friend Nadia leans closer and whispers, "Is it just me, or is Hudson Tanner looking at you like you're his dessert?"

A shiver runs down my spine at the possibility.

The very dangerous possibility.

"And he's going to eat me with a cherry on top," I murmur back.

Nadia fans her face. "*Someone* has an elaborate fantasy," she teases softly.

And the thing is . . . I do.

I have, ever since I met him a year ago at a charity event, shortly after I moved to town. Hudson introduced himself in a voice like honey and whiskey that sent sparks straight between my legs.

But it isn't his voice alone. It's what he does with it, the words that fall from his tongue when he's near me. The man is an incorrigible flirt. The ultimate charmer. And he seems determined to get me into bed.

"Maybe," I tell Nadia. "But I have a baseball team to turn around, and the last thing I need is a distraction, especially one who's my rival, wrapped in a custom-made tux."

"Bet you're thinking how he'd look out of that tux," she teases.

I give a little shrug and reach for my glass of champagne, meeting my friend's knowing gaze. "I am. I definitely am. And I should absolutely stop."

She tips her glass to mine, clinking. "But will you?"

I draw a deep breath. "That's an excellent question."

But if I do stop, it won't be now because Hudson's walking in my direction with purposeful strides.

Intensity etches his strong jawline, and determination darkens his deep brown eyes.

Hudson Tanner drips with sex appeal, money, and cocky charm.

And I won't be swayed. My focus is on my team and only my team.

Though my surging pulse suggests otherwise.

HUDSON

My single-minded goal since I met Marlow has been to take her home with me.

To spend the night with this brunette beauty who has curves for days.

She's everything that revs my engine. She's fire and brilliance. She has a sharp mind, a ruthless competitive heart, and a mouth made for sin.

And tonight, she'll be mine.

I cross the ballroom with that in mind, weaving my way to the siren in the gold dress that clings to her irresistible shape. She tries to look away, but it's futile. Her fierce, green-eyed gaze swings around the room then settles again on me.

My path takes me by some of my players here tonight—Crosby Cash, my third baseman; Chance Ashford, my closer; Grant Blackwood, my catcher. These guys do me proud—they won a World Series for me last fall, and I sure as hell enjoy the ring on my finger.

"Good to see you," I tell Grant as I pass. Then to Chance, "Hope you're having a great night." Crosby gets a "See you at spring training soon."

But I've got Marlow in my crosshairs the whole time.

When I'm ten feet away, her friend peels away.

I stop, standing next to Marlow, my rival and the object of all my desires. This woman who's resisted all my flirtation. But that's going to change tonight. Because she may act impervious to this spark between us, but I have a wager to offer her, one I bet Marlow Winters will find irresistible.

"What a pleasure to see you, Marlow," I say.

Her fingers touch her throat. "It's always good to see you, Hudson."

"You look absolutely . . . enchanting," I tell her.

"That's exactly what I was going for," she deadpans.

"No doubt," I say dryly.

"And you're so very debonair."

I run a finger down the lapel of my jacket, my eyes pinned on the woman I crave. It's simple, in some ways, this desire. The moment I met Marlow at a charity luncheon last year, my pulse spiked and my blood heated. But the more I got to know her, the higher the desire spiraled. She's intensely competitive—something I learned at a team owner's meeting in Las Vegas last month.

We played poker until well past midnight, betting, then betting some more. By the end of the night, after she'd cleaned up at the table, she gathered her winnings, winked, and said good night.

She's everything I want under me.

How to win her is the question, and I'm pretty sure that competitive streak is the answer.

I glance around the room, grandly decorated for the occasion. "I see both our teams and players are up for some awards tonight."

She stares at me like I've casually mentioned that water is wet, which of course, figuratively, I have.

"Yes, Hudson. They are. Best Sportsmanship, Best Comeback, Excellence in Performance. The list goes on," she says, flicking some strands of that lush chestnut hair from her shoulders.

"Indeed, it does," I agree, not so subtly running my forefinger on my right hand over the World Series ring on my left.

Marlow's gaze swings to the thing she covets the most.

Victory.

And the symbol of it.

Yes, Marlow, I've got a ring. I know you want one.

Which leads me to this . . . "How about we place a bet?"

She nibbles at the bait. "On what, exactly?"

I nod to the stage where the presentation will take place. "Whose team wins the most awards."

She raises her chin, her lips parting in a smile. "So easy, Hudson. You know I'll win. You must want to lose."

"I never want to lose," I say.

Unless it's a bet with a fantastic woman.

"What are the stakes? That ring you can't stop taunting me with?"

"Oh, does it bother you that I have one?"

"Not in the least," she retorts.

She's lying. I can see it in the set of her jaw. Of course she's lying, because of course she wants this.

"Great," I say. "Then when my team wins more, why don't you join me for a nightcap? We can take my limo. Have some champagne."

"And why do you want that? A drink with me?"

I don't mince words, and I don't play coy. That's not who I am.

I lift a hand, roam my fingers along the soft strands of her hair, then lay my desire on the line. "Because I want you, Marlow. I have since I met you. I want to show you how good I can make you feel."

She's quiet for a few seconds, her lips parting, her skin flushing. It's a gorgeous look, the color rising from her breasts up her chest to her throat, where she teased me moments ago with her fingers.

A throat I want to kiss and lick.

"What makes you think I might want that?" Her question comes out breathy.

I give an easy shrug. "Hope. Just hope."

As I let go of her hair, she studies my face, gaging whether I'm serious. "And if my team wins the tally?"

"Well, what would you like?" I ask easily.

She hums, her eyes twinkling. "Your closing pitcher."

A laugh bursts from me. "Chance Ashford isn't for sale."

She shrugs, turns away. "Then I'm not sure you have anything I want."

Oh, I bet I do.

Time to show her I'm determined. "You can have my limo. I know you like it. You mentioned as much when we played cards."

Her eyes twinkle. "I do like your stretch limo, and I need a new one." After a token pause for consideration, she extends a hand, and we shake. "It's a bet."

An hour later, my team cleans up, my players winning four awards to her two.

3

MARLOW

Three words.

I want you.

They echo in my mind all through the gala.

They sweep down my body, become an aching pulse between my legs.

That daring, tempting man.

The man who makes me hot, who winds me up, who . . . wants me.

I can't possibly consider a tryst with the owner of the city's *other* baseball team. You don't play bedroom games with your competitor, with the man who's gunning for the same prize and the same fans, day in and day out.

But I never renege on a bet, so when the fête winds down, I gather my wrap, meet my rival at the door, and we walk down the steps to his waiting limo.

Hudson slides in after me and thanks the driver, who then shuts the door.

A bottle of champagne chills on ice. Cristal. My favorite brand.

Music pipes through the sound system—Sam Smith. My favorite artist.

A small table pops out of the console. A deck of cards lies on the black velvet surface, alongside a stack of chips.

Someone well and truly has my number.

"Interesting, Hudson. I see you've got all my favorite things," I say as the car pulls away from the Luxe Hotel.

His grin is sly—devilish in fact. Just this side of satisfied. "I pay attention, Marlow."

He lifts the bottle, asks with his eyes if he can pour it.

"I do love champagne," I say.

His eyes twinkle. "Like I said—I pay attention."

He pours two flutes, then hands me one, and we clink glasses. "To this limo you covet."

I scoff. "I wouldn't say *covet*."

"What would you say?"

I run a hand along the buttery leather seat. "It's simply a car. I have my own." I knock back some of the bubbly.

"But you like mine. Especially since I have all the things you like in it," he says.

Which makes me wonder. "Did you know you were going to win?"

He wiggles a brow.

My jaw drops. "How did you know?"

"I didn't say I knew."

I set down the glass, building up a head of steam.

"You got an inside tip, I bet. From the network. That's why you had all these . . . accouterments," I say, gesturing around the limo. "I can't believe you deceived me."

Then, with a quick burst of anger, I reach for his bow tie, grab it, tug it hard. "You tricked me."

And I'm . . . closer than I've ever been to Hudson Tanner. I catch a quick whiff of his expensive cologne, and the woodsy cedar scent goes to my head, mixes with the taste of the champagne.

"I wanted to win," he says without an ounce of guilt. With only . . . pleasure.

"So badly you got a tip just to snag a ride with me?"

His dark gaze holds mine, his eyes shimmering with desire and intensity. With gamesmanship. "I want what I want. And I want you," he says, all low and gravelly and far too sexy. A shiver runs down my spine, and I simply won't let go of his tie. Because I want him too. And I haven't been able to eradicate this craving.

Perhaps the way over it is through it.

I tug him toward me, our lips perilously close. "Then take a kiss," I hiss.

"With pleasure," he says, and he seals his mouth to mine.

His lips claim me.

They sweep over mine as he takes my mouth, and my whole damn sense of control. He's commanding and powerful, kissing deep and hard. His hand slides into my hair, curls around my skull, and he holds me in place.

I'm made only of arousal.

Of wild desire, so strong it has its own pulse, its own heartbeat.

Just once.

Just tonight.

Just in this limo.

As his lips explore mine, he murmurs and moans, his tongue stroking inside my mouth, and all my systems go into overdrive.

My skin sizzles, and I'm hot everywhere.

He breaks away to say, "Let me kiss you between those gorgeous legs. Let me make you come hard on my lips."

I blame Sam Smith. As the chorus to his tune plays, I'm enrapt, enthralled by my rival. "You have five minutes," I tell him.

He stares at me, his eyes smoldering and full of desire. "Consider it done."

I'm vibrating with lust as he stretches me out, pushes up my skirt, spreads my legs.

"Mmm. Nothing underneath, Marlow. How did I know you'd be this daring?" he says, hooking my legs over his shoulders.

"I like to take risks."

And then I shut the hell up when the man in the tux presses his full, lush lips to my pussy, kissing me like I am all the desserts.

I'm going to go off like a rocket. He already has me so on edge, racing toward the finish line.

He presses his mouth against me, and I groan. Nothing has ever felt like this, like he's worshiping me. His moans are obscene and alluring at the same time as he licks and kisses and sends me flying.

Soon, my legs are shaking and I'm falling, breaking.

As I come down from the high, he crawls up me and whispers in my ear, "Next time we make a bet, I want you to come on my cock."

Then he takes me to my home, presses a kiss on top of my hand, and says goodnight.

I go inside.

What the hell just happened?

4

HUDSON

The Start of the Season

Romance is like baseball.

You have to be in it for the whole damn season.

For the endless stretch of 162 games.

That's what I do.

Whenever I cross paths with Marlow during the season, our games continue. As I make opportunities to see her more often, our bets increase. We up the ante.

We don't bet on outcomes of games. And we never bet on who'll win on the field.

But our wagers are related.

Whose team will have better attendance. Whose team will win the fan vote for best new uniforms. Who'll sell the most jerseys at the team store.

Our games are sex games.

Bedroom bets.

Illicit trysts.

When the Dragons beat the Cougars in the series, and surpasses the attendance from last year's series, she wins my limo fair and square, and I have it delivered to her mansion.

That night, she swings by my ballpark, lowers the window of my erstwhile automobile, and asks if I need a ride.

When I get in, I've hardly closed the door before she pounces on me, shoves off my jacket, unzips my pants, and frees my cock.

"What got you so hard so quickly, Hudson?" she asks.

The way this gorgeous woman wants to devour my dick, that's what. "You. Just you."

"You do want me," she murmurs.

"I want you to suck my cock. Take me deep, Marlow. Make it so I don't regret losing this car to you."

Getting on her knees, she licks a stripe up the underside of my dick. "You don't regret anything except bad trades and losing games," she says, then draws the head between her lips, licking and sucking with fervor.

"I bet you can finish me off in two minutes. That'd give me plenty of time to eat your sweet pussy for a good, long while," I tell her.

And that gets Marlow going.

I've never met a woman who loves being licked more than Marlow. She craves it shamelessly, demands oral loving from me, throws down crazy bets with her sweet, hot center as the prize.

But tonight, she treats my cock like a treat, sucking me down, licking my hard length with long, intense swirls, drawing me deep, so damn deep I hit the back of her throat.

My body shudders. My thighs shake, and the billionaire I crave takes my cock all the way into her mouth, lavishing blissful attention all along it as pleasure rumbles through my body, taking over my world.

The heady promise of a climax blasts through my cells as I grip her head, fuck her mouth, and warn her. "Coming now. Take it all."

And she does, like a beautifully obedient rival on her knees as I come down her throat.

A little later, we play another game of poker as we cruise over the Golden Gate Bridge.

"What's it going to be this time?" she asks, sweeping her arm out to indicate our wheels. "Since I already won your favorite car."

I laugh lightly, shaking my head. "This isn't my favorite, honey."

She arches a brow. "It's not?"

I lean in close, cup her cheek, and whisper softly against her face, "I got a cherry-red Bugatti last week. That one's my favorite."

She hums, her eyes narrowing. "Then I want that. And you can have my condo in Napa."

Color me intrigued.

She does have a stunning condo overlooking a vineyard.

"This time, we bet on the playoffs," I say, feeling

confident. After all, I own the reigning World Series champions. Surely, we'll not only bring in the fans, but sell more beer. A bet on beer—yes, that feels just right. "The owner of whichever team sells the most wins."

* * *

October . . .

Nine runs.

Nine fucking runs.

We lose game six of the divisionals by a rout.

I put on my best *there's always next year* face as I leave the ballpark, say goodnight to some of the players in the lot, then I stop in my tracks.

Outside the ballpark, my old limo is idling.

Marlow leans against the side of it, wearing a short skirt, high heels, and a red silk blouse. She looks devilishly pleased.

No wonder.

She's about to get another car from me. Turns out, fans of losing teams don't want much beer. Guess they'll drown their sorrows in other ways.

In her hand, she holds a bottle of Cristal. Raises it. "Should have sold champagne, Hudson. Maybe try that next time. But I thought I'd make it easy for you." With her other hand, she pats the side of my—dammit, *her*—limo. "Decided to give you a ride. We can go fetch your Bugatti now. And I even brought champagne to toast to my Dragons going further than your Cougars."

Goddammit. She's so sexy it's killing me, even when she's full-on gloating.

I stride right up to her.

"You taunt me, Marlow. You make me want to kiss you madly—right here, so everyone knows you get on your knees for your rival."

She lifts her chin. "You wouldn't dare."

I scoff, reaching up to run my thumb along her jawline. "I think you know I'm up for any dare."

She stares at me, refusing to break eye contact. "I dare you to tie me up and fuck me in the back of . . . *my* limo as you take me to your Bugatti."

I reach for the door, open it. "Get inside. I'm going to claim *my* prize."

5

MARLOW

I wore this skirt for a reason.

In one minute, it's bunched up around my waist.

My wrists are bound above my head, knotted with his silk tie.

And Hudson slides his long, thick shaft inside me.

Ruthlessly, the way I like it.

"Fuck me hard, Hudson. Make me scream," I tell him as a sharp, hot spike of pleasure hits my center.

I ache for more.

More fucking.

More orgasms.

More games.

Roughly, he grabs my thighs, digs his fingers into my flesh, and hikes my leg around his hips.

And he goes deeper.

He fucks me without mercy as we cruise through the city on the way to my brand-new car.

I let out a long, lingering moan. "I'm thinking of my new sports car," I murmur, taunting him.

"I'll fuck you in that too," he growls.

"You better," I say.

And then words cease as we drive through San Francisco and he drives relentlessly into me, sending me into a world of lust and heat and passion. I come ridiculously hard. He groans like an animal, unleashing himself inside me.

Panting my name.

Whispering in my ear.

"You're so fucking sexy," he murmurs.

I press a soft kiss to his face. "So are you."

We straighten up, adjusting clothes, making ourselves presentable as we roll along Columbus Avenue in North Beach.

When I glance to my side, I spot a familiar couple on the streets. "Isn't that Sullivan Fitzgerald and Erin Madison?" I point out the tinted window.

He peers in the same direction. "Normally, I'd want to talk to him after a game."

I laugh. "Do I distract you from chatting with your players?"

Hudson turns back to me, those dark eyes flaming with desire. "You do. You distract and fascinate," he says, pouring bubbly for us, handing me a glass. "So much that I can't get you out of my head. Haven't all year. Haven't since the gala. You're the only woman I think about."

His words are dangerous, because they make my heart want to get closer to him.

That's the true risk, isn't it?

"Surely, there are others," I say.

His gaze holds mine. "You're the only one."

My breath hitches. "It's the same for me."

Something shifts then, and we don't go to his home right away. We drive and talk, and we get to know each other. I learn more about the man behind the tux, the man who likes to fuck and bet and win.

And when we reach his home, I invite him back to mine.

That is, if he's willing to ride shotgun in my brand-new Bugatti.

6

MARLOW

Late Fall

The off-season isn't off for me at all.

It's wildly busy with trades and deals.

My team made it further in the playoffs, but not far enough. I have the big bats, like Holden Kingsley and Declan Steele, and I have a fantastic catcher in Drew McBride. I have some great starting pitchers too.

But I covet more aces.

That's always what you need in this game—the starters who can go the distance on the mound, and then the one who can shut the motherfucking door.

I want a World Series desperately.

I want it with an ache that lives deep in my bones.

So, I spend my days working with my general manager to find the right fireman to close out our games.

And I spend my nights in the limo with Hudson.

Sometimes, though, we take my Bugatti, and we drive up to Wine Country. But we don't dine at Napa's three-star restaurants.

Turns out we both like dive bars.

And burger joints.

Napa has plenty of those too.

Hudson also likes to play pool. What do you know? So do I. And I'm better at it than he is.

So, one night, we play for tips.

Insider trade tips.

When I beat him, I set my chin on the cue, and tell him to give me his best trade tip. He scratches his jaw, beckons me closer, so close I catch a whiff of the cedar scent that drives me wild. "There's literally nothing I can do with this intel since I already have an all-star closer, but Shane Walker from the Comets is on the trading block."

I roll my eyes. "Tell me something I don't know."

"Aww, you thought that's what I would do? Give you a real tip?"

"So now we play for fake tips?"

"We can play for players, for cars, for homes. Never for tips," he says.

That's fair. I wouldn't have given him one either.

But I do give him a blow job that night on the side of the road.

And in the morning, I finish the deal I started a few weeks ago—trading for Shane Walker.

* * *

Soon, my nights with Hudson grow longer, turning into mornings too.

The man can make excellent pancakes, and I do like carbs at sunrise. I also like orgasms, so we strike a deal.

He can spend the nights if he gives me both.

And he does.

In fact, I like our nights and our mornings, our bets and our sex, our barbs and our fire so much that I don't want to stop.

He hasn't distracted me one bit from my work.

He's energized me.

The competition fires me up. The desire to beat my lover at the game of baseball motivates me every day.

But there's something else I want.

One night in January, after he shoves me onto his cock, tells me to ride him reverse cowgirl in my limo, and makes me come so hard I see stars, I challenge him to poker as we cruise along the 101.

"I have new stakes this time," I tell him as I deal.

"Lay it on me," he says.

"If I win, I want you to bring my favorite comedian to town."

He furrows his brow, parts his lips, but says nothing.

I've surprised him as I hoped I would.

"Why would you want that?" he finally asks.

"I like Matilda Barker. I want to see her perform. If I win, you'll get her for me, and take me on a date."

The grin that spreads on his face is easy, clever, and knowing.

He loses the game, and he does it deliberately.

It's as obvious as my desire to date him for real.

7

HUDSON

On Valentine's Day, I swing by Marlow's mansion in my new wheels—a sleek, white limo that's longer than hers.

I head to her gate, enter my code, and walk up the steps right as she opens the front door.

Beautiful.

She's all casual but still sexy as fuck in jeans and a tight red sweater with buttons I want to tear off with my teeth.

"I have something you'll want to see," I tell her.

I take her hand, and she lets out an appreciative murmur. "Who knew you were a hand holder?"

"Who knew you loved comedy clubs?"

She brings her finger to her red lips. "Keep my secrets, Hudson."

"I do, honey. I absolutely do."

She jerks on my hand, stops in her tracks in front of my car. "You. Did. Not."

I shoot her a crooked grin. "Like my new limo?"

She growls. "It's bigger than mine."

"Huh. What do you know? It is."

She shakes her head at me. "You always try to beat me."

"And you wouldn't have it any other way. Plus, there's more room to fuck you hard in this limo. Just the way you like it."

That's what I do on the drive to the comedy club for the date I arranged for her, to see the comic I brought to town.

Once there, I savor every second of Marlow's laughter, of her company.

During the set, I gesture subtly at some of the other patrons and whisper in her ear. "I see your new closer, your catcher, and one of my pitchers," I say softly, eyeing the table with Shane Walker, Drew McBride, and Sullivan Fitzgerald.

Her gaze follows mine. "I noticed. And they can't seem to keep their eyes off that table of gorgeous women."

"Bet we're not the only ones fucking tonight," I tell her.

"Bet they all are," she whispers.

"Too bad we can't bet on that, though, since we'll be too busy enjoying ourselves to see what happens."

"Then how about we both bet on orgasms in your limo tonight?"

I lean back in my chair, laughing, then tug her close. "Honey, that's a guarantee."

THE END

DOG FISHING

AN EPILOGUE

NOVA

Here's the truest thing of all—looks fade, but humor lasts.

Don't get me wrong.

I love a hot babe as much as the next woman.

But the way to my heart and my panties is definitely through my funny bone.

Tonight, though, let's start with panties, since I wouldn't mind getting in *hers*.

The ones belonging to that sexy, clever, naughty gal on the stage.

The woman making me laugh with her dog-fishing jokes.

Matilda's careful with pronouns. She doesn't use them at first, just says *they* as she strides across the stage, her mic in hand. But I've got a feeling she likes the same things I do.

"This last date I went on was great. When I said sit, they sat. When I said come . . ." She stops, flashes a grin at the audience. "Oh, please. It happens that way in romance novels. When the man goes all alpha commanding in bed and says 'Come for me.'" The adorable, curly-haired comic with the big eyes and bow-shaped lips smiles coyly. "And the woman's like 'Oh yes, yes, yes' As if that works."

She turns the other way, taking a beat, then finishing. "I don't know, though, because it never worked that way for me. But if a tall, commanding, hot AF *badass babe* said that to me?" Matilda begins . . . and I blink.

Did she just use the name of my podcast?

I mean, it's not a unique name, per se.

But still, it *is* the name of my show.

I sit up straighter, skin tingling.

"Then, I just might," Matilda adds with a sly smile thrown my way. Or maybe I just want to catch it.

And *her.*

"So that's why it took me longer to break up with that gal. Her dog was too adorable. He sat on command and came when called and was basically perf. But I learned a valuable lesson." She wags her finger. "Fall for the person before the pooch."

When the set ends, I chat with my friends for a few minutes, but not too long. As soon as Matilda makes her way from backstage and into the lounge area, I'm up on my high-heeled boots, heading to her.

"I have a dog you might fall for," I tell her.

"Oh, do you now?" she says, so fucking cute and adorable. "A Great Dane, I bet?"

I laugh. "Or maybe a Mastiff."

She laughs too. "Are you going to show me a pic?"

I grab my phone, open the photos, and show her a shot of my Border Collie mix.

Matilda coos then meets my gaze. "But you're-dog fishing me now, aren't you?"

I wiggle a brow. "So, it's working, then? It's making you want me? The dog pics?"

Matilda thoughtfully screws up the corner of her lips, eyes me up and down. "I wouldn't say the dog pics did it. But they help. What truly did it was that . . . you're *the* badass babe."

I laugh, a little vindicated, then I let down my guard. "Do you really listen to my show?"

Matilda gives me the flirtiest eyes I've ever seen. "I recognized you in the audience from your pic on your podcast site. Dropped that line in just for you."

And my nipples tingle.

"So maybe *I* was fishing for *you*, Nova Badass Babe," Matilda says.

I tip my forehead to the bar. "Can I buy you a drink?"

She slides an arm around my waist. "You can definitely buy me a drink. And maybe more."

At the bar, Matilda asks for a bourbon on the rocks, and I think I might be a little bit in love.

"Not to be a copycat, but I'll have the same," I tell the blonde bartender.

"Coming right up," she says in a pretty British accent, then to Matilda, she adds, "And thank you for bringing the crowds tonight. You were fantastic."

"It was my pleasure," she says. When the bartender

leaves, Matilda gives me a naughty stare. "Bet that won't be my *only* pleasure."

I laugh, set a hand on her arm, and whisper in my best sultry voice, "I can promise you that."

An hour later, we're in a Lyft, kissing like crazy, hands sliding into hair, making out.

And then, back at my place, we're doing a whole lot more.

* * *

The next day, I meet my lady-pack for coffee. Turns out we all got some good loving on Valentine's Day.

And six weeks later, I take my girlfriend, Matilda, to a baseball game as my friends watch their guys play.

"To think, you almost fell for me just because of my dog," I say, and I kiss her cheek.

She kisses me back. "Well, I do like your dog. But I like you too, Nova."

That works for me.

It definitely works for me.

And it looks like Valentine's Day worked for everyone.

It makes me wonder if it's Cupid bringing us together. What cinches the idea, though, is how when my gaze swings to the owner's box, Marlow Winters is kissing Hudson Tanner.

Kissing like maybe they're in love now too.

Just like the rest of us.

THE END

I can't wait to share my next sports romance with you! Don't miss the sexy single dad football star Harlan and his forbidden romance with jilted bride Katie! It's coming your way in A Wild Card Kiss! Here's a sexy preview!

Holy smokes.

She is a sight.

As sexy as Katie was more than seven years ago, she's somehow even more stunning today. Her hair is all done up and clipped back, with lush, dark blonde strands curling over her shoulders. Her skin shimmers. Her high cheekbones slant in fantastic contrast to her pert, freckled nose.

The last seven years have been very good to her.

And yet, everything about the woman is incongruous. It's not a stretch to imagine there's something wildly wrong tonight. A woman doesn't wear a wedding dress solo to a bowling alley bar on a Saturday night in July without a reason. But I don't want to make any assumptions. Hell, her groom might be in the little boys' room, taking care of business.

Or waxing a big old bowling ball.

Or playing a speed sesh of Pac-Man in the video game lounge.

But a quick glance around tells me she's not here with the mister after saying *I do*. The place is mostly empty with just a few groups of old dudes in bowling shirts left of the crowd, and no one who looks like he got hitched today. So I'm thinking Katie and her man didn't rush off to Pinup Lanes for an ironic game of bowling to celebrate their nuptials.

Just to be safe, though, I go in nice and easy. I'd like to avoid hitting on another man's bride.

What am I saying? I'm not going to hit on her, period. I'm merely saying hello to an old flame.

I close the distance, leaning a hip against the bar. "Hello, blast from the past. And happy . . . Saturday night?" I arch a brow, give a crooked smile, hoping maybe that's the start of what she needs. A friendly face. Someone to lighten the mood.

Katie turns to me in slow motion, taking her sweet time. Her blue eyes are edged with sadness and fury. But when they lock on mine, recognition sparks, and a wide range of emotions dances across her face.

Surprise. Embarrassment. And maybe a touch of excitement?

"Or we can be more precise and call it Happy Just-Escaped-Marriage-To-A-Cheater day," she deadpans.

Whoa.

Someone does not mince words.

Who the hell would do that to her?

I blow out a long stream of air and scrub a hand over my jaw. "They ought to have cards for that," I say, trying to match her mood. "Say goodbye to the double-cross-ing, duplicitous dick."

She lifts her shot glass, a tiny laugh escaping her lips. "Yes. And the inside could say *Congratulations to the jilted bride*," she says, hurt leaking into her tone now.

My heart screams for her. "I hate that this happened to you, but I'm glad you got out in the nick of time." I park myself on a stool and do the one useful thing I can —I lift two fingers at the bartender. "I'll take a shot too."

"Coming right up," he says.

I turn to Katie. "I cannot let you drink alone. Not on your wedding night. It's just not right. I refuse to do it. So you have a *just escaped marriage to the traitor* drinking buddy."

She pats the bar, heaving a sigh. "Then drink up, partner."

The bartender slides over a tequila for me. "Here you go, sir."

I slap down some bills. "And I'll take care of her bar tab tonight," I say.

Katie shakes her head. "I've got it."

I scoff, patting my chest. "Gentleman here. It's the least I can do on your Great Escape Day."

She holds up her hand in surrender. "I have no argument left in me. Thank you."

"You are most welcome. And by the way, on behalf of all men everywhere, I'd like to apologize for whatever that dickhead of a guy did. He is clearly an asshat of the highest order, and he does not deserve you. That's just a fact."

She lifts her glass in agreement, then downs the shot. "He is, but that's not the worst of it, Harlan."

"Oh, you remember my name?" I tease before I knock back my drink too.

She narrows her eyes, shoots me a *c'mon* look. "Did you think I wouldn't?"

"I'm just happy you did . . . *Katie*." It comes out

flirtier than I expected. But maybe flirting is what she needs tonight?

Her blue eyes widen. "Are you trying to impress me by remembering mine?"

"Did that impress you? If so, check out the other details I remember." I count off on my fingers. "You're from Texas, you love fashion and flirting, and I sorely missed the chance for a second date with you."

I put that last nugget out there because . . . why the hell not? Maybe tonight is the perfect time to let the woman know she was wanted something fierce.

Katie shoots me a skeptical glance. "Now you're just blowing smoke up my skirt."

"I assure you, no smoke is being blown. But I do like your skirt." I curl my fingers to beckon the rest of the story from her. "Go on. You were about to tell me what is the worst part of today. Also, if you need to punch anyone or anything, my chest is a brick wall." I pat my pecs, inviting her to toss her fist my way. "Feel free to take it out on me."

Another small laugh falls from her lips, and I feel like I'm winning at something—at making a woman who's had a terrible day feel a tiny bit better.

Katie breathes deep, yoga-style, like she's inhaling a *namaste* to form the next words: "I walked in on the groom kissing the mother of the bride."

What?

The revelation spins my head around, horror-movie style, with shocked disbelief.

That can't be true.

"Tell me that's a joke," I say. Because how could it be anything else?

She sighs and shakes her head, her lips quivering slightly. My heart lurches toward her.

"I'm not joking," she says in a terribly sad whisper.

I can't resist giving her some comfort. I reach for her arm, squeeze it, rub my palm along her soft skin. "That is the worst. People *say* things are the worst—bad parking spot, terrible coffee. But this scenario is the actual worst, and I am so damn sorry it happened to you."

"Thank you. I really appreciate that. My friends and my dad tried to help comfort me today. They were helpful, but even though I asked them to leave, when they did I discovered I didn't want to be home either. So I wandered around the city alone until I stumbled across this place. It seemed"—she stops to survey the retro room—"fitting in some way. It's the complete opposite of my wedding." She plucks at the fabric of her dress. "Maybe that's why I left this on. To wear it for a completely opposite purpose. Just for me on a random night."

What she's saying makes perfect sense. "You're reclaiming it in a way."

She seems to consider that, then nods. "Yes, maybe I am."

I point to the door. "Did you want to be alone? It'll be hard for me to go, because there's a part of me that doesn't feel like I can abandon you. But if you need to be alone, I'll leave."

Her eyes drift down to my hand on her arm. "No. Actually, I don't want to be alone."

Grab A Wild Card Kiss while it's on sale!

Be sure to sign up for my mailing list to be the first to know when swoony, sexy new romances are available or on sale!

ALSO BY LAUREN BLAKELY

FULL PACKAGE, the #1 New York Times Bestselling romantic comedy!

BIG ROCK, the hit New York Times Bestselling standalone romantic comedy!

THE SEXY ONE, a New York Times Bestselling standalone romance!

THE KNOCKED UP PLAN, a multi-week USA Today and Amazon Charts Bestselling standalone romance!

MOST VALUABLE PLAYBOY, a sexy multi-week USA Today Bestselling sports romance! And its companion sports romance, MOST LIKELY TO SCORE!

WANDERLUST, a USA Today Bestselling contemporary romance!

COME AS YOU ARE, a Wall Street Journal and multi-week USA Today Bestselling contemporary romance!

PART-TIME LOVER, a multi-week USA Today Bestselling contemporary romance!

UNBREAK MY HEART, an emotional second chance USA Today Bestselling contemporary romance!

BEST LAID PLANS, a sexy friends-to-lovers USA Today Bestselling romance!

The Heartbreakers! The USA Today and WSJ Bestselling rock star series of standalone!

P.S. IT'S ALWAYS BEEN YOU, a sweeping, second chance romance!

MY ONE WEEK HUSBAND, a sexy standalone romance!

CONTACT

I love hearing from readers! You can find me on Twitter at LaurenBlakely3, Instagram at LaurenBlakelyBooks, Facebook at LaurenBlakelyBooks, or online at Lauren-Blakely.com. You can also email me at laurenblakelybooks@gmail.com

Printed in Great Britain
by Amazon